Home to the Cowboy's Arms

Home to the Cowboy's Arms

Destiny's River

Debra Holt

TULE
PUBLISHING

Home to the Cowboy's Arms

Tule Publishing First Printing, January 2025

The Tule Publishing, Inc.

First Publication by Tule Publishing 2025

Cover design by Lee Hyat Designs

ISBN: 978-1-965640-11-1

Dear Readers....

Welcome to the first book in my latest series...**Destiny's River**. This is a special series following the road to romance and forever homes for four siblings who grew up together in foster care. Each finds their own way into the world and eventually all roads will lead them to that special place in all our hearts and minds... home.

Home means different things to different people. But it is always a wish that begins in our minds and grows in our hearts. And people are the heart of home wherever it might be and whatever it might look like for each person. It is my hope that when reading this series, something along the way might remind you of that special dream or place you have found or may still search for in your own story.

For me, home is my family and loved ones first and foremost. May you enjoy this trip to Destiny's River and the stories found there!

Happy Reading,
Debra Holt
August, 2024

Prologue

"HUSH CRYING, CASSIE. Things will get better. We're going to find a home. We'll have a family. If we can't find one that wants us…then we'll make one for ourselves. All of us." The house was quiet in the late hour. Others had gone to bed, but the two sisters huddled on the back porch steps, cloaked in the silence of the yard lit by the silver glow of the full moon overhead.

"What do we know about making a home? None of us have had one of those…not really. And where? Where is this home?"

"It's where your heart is," Tori whispered. "That's what Granny said when she had her right mind. She was smart and kind…she just got too old. So, I figure she knew better than most. Lots of people say that—I read it before and heard it on television once. So, we'll use that to find our place and make it that way."

"Promise?"

"I promise. I've always looked out for all of us and that will never stop."

And Tori had kept that promise. She aged out of the foster system first. The money saved working after school and on weekends had been used in part to buy a seat on a bus leaving Baton Rouge, and she headed out with an old, donated suitcase and a mound of determination. Failure would not be an option. She was the first to set foot into the realm known as freedom—her sister and two brothers would be right behind her. They needed to know where *home* was. Her gaze locked on the vista outside the bus's window. Her first decision was which way to go.

No reason to go but in one direction: west. That choice was made for no other reason than she loved sunsets and figured there would be more spaces to find a place to have a good view of one and find a likely home in places that weren't so crowded already. And when she had stepped off the bus at the next-to-last stop on her ticket, she heard that voice inside her say she just might have found the place.

Something had made her take note of her surroundings as she nibbled her food on the park bench. And there was an omen—two as a matter of fact. One was that the light had changed to a warm glowing orange. The clouds in the sky seemed to reflect it and created a patchwork quilt of warmth and welcoming, slowing the approach of dusk. And to seal the deal, while she sat on the bench contemplating the amazing beauty, a small mewing sound had come from the bank of bushes beside her. Upon careful inspection, there was a tiny face, one that seemed too big for the rest of its body, which didn't amount to much at all. Huge gold eyes watched her with wariness, yet hunger was the predominant interest. In fact, when she had picked up the little creature, it was light as a feather on the breeze. Clearly, it had smelled the half of a bologna sandwich she had saved from her lunch to have as dinner, being economical with her funds.

"Okay, little one, you just might need this last bit of

food more than me." She handed it over and sat both on the bench beside her. The cat gobbled the bit of food down in nothing flat and looked for more.

"We'll get more soon enough," she said and scooped him up, where he seemed to settle into her palm against her chest with relief. She wasn't alone. Neither did it seem either was the kitten. The sign above the bus station creaked in the breeze.

"Destiny's River," she read, the words rolling off her tongue for the first time. Tori stood and looked around once more. It seemed to be a quiet place. Lights blinked red and then green along the street she could see from her position. A few ranch vehicles had passed during her time sitting there. And a couple of passersby had even smiled at her. That didn't often happen…if at all…where she had come from. People kept their heads down and their smiles hidden from view. They hurried. Here, looked like people just walked, maybe even strolled.

After Tori and her siblings had been given over to their grandmother to raise when they were just a little more than toddlers, they had been moved to Alabama. She had heard stories of when her parents had met in Texas and married. Her father had been an oilfield worker. Her mother had worked days as a waitress and nights as a cleaning lady in offices. A neighbor had been their surrogate parent/babysitter. Then fate had sent them all from Texas to Alabama after their dad took off to parts unknown and their grandmother was taken by cancer.

She took a few moments to breathe in the approaching early evening and memorize her first sunset in Texas and possible new hometown. The sidewalks were clean and there were even planter boxes every few feet and she could imagine them filled with flowers in the spring. Oak trees were in abundance on the green spaces. It was a place that seemed to invite one to stay a while and search out hidden treasures in the shops she had seen coming into the town. It could be a postcard that one might expect of a place one called home. *Home.*

Tori tucked the kitten closer inside the denim jacket she had on and went inside the station. The ticket agent looked up and gave her a kind smile and a nod. She asked for the refund for the rest of the ticket and got it, along with another smile.

"You visiting here, miss? Have relations meeting you?" It didn't seem intrusive, so Tori returned the smile.

"I don't really know about staying yet. I might take a look around. Do you know if any of those stores I saw as the bus came into town might be looking for help?"

"I see. Well, you won't find a better place to stay for a while. Folks round these parts are pretty welcoming." She paused. "I'm thinking there might be two or three places that could do with more help. And if you're in need of a place to stay, you give a stop at this address," and she was jotting down something on the slip of bright pink paper. Then she handed it over. "That's my cousin Addie's boarding house. I'm Birdie McGraw, by the way. You go three blocks past the courthouse on the square. Turn left at the gazebo at the edge of the big lawn and go one block and it's a cute older house with bright green shutters. She might have a little space open. And she'll know I sent you, so she'll give you a good deal. Her prices are the best in town."

"Thank you, I will certainly check with her." Tori thought of something else before she turned away. "Do you know if anyone might be looking for this little kitten?" She pushed the cloth back a bit and the kitten landed its wide-eyed stare on the older woman.

"That little one showed up here with a couple of others—probably litter mates—about four…five days ago. Made themselves a place in the bushes. I might have left a few nibbles for them here and there, but this isn't a place for little ones like that…too busy with traffic during the day. And I think the other two might have found homes. Haven't seen them around for the last couple of days. This little one is on his own."

That was all she needed to verify. Tori nodded. "Guess the next thing is to find a place that not only takes in humans but a straggly kitten, too."

The woman named Birdie grinned. "Well, you won't get any grief from Addie. She has had a neon sign out for all sorts of critters most of her life. Seems you two are partners now. Good luck to you both. Don't be a stranger. I'm here most days."

The woman's kindness enhanced the warmth of the early evening's glow inside her. And when she located the house with the green shutters, a strange yet peaceful feeling settled over her. She stood outside the garden gate for a couple minutes.

"Well, have you made up your mind?" came the voice from one of the rockers on the deep front porch. A woman, white haired, with round-rimmed glasses sat forward a bit and settled her gaze upon her.

"Pardon me?"

"That gate opens up nicely. Best come up and sit a spell. View of that Texas sunset only gets better from one of these rockers."

Chapter One

TORI PUSHED HERSELF up from the comfy cushion seat of the high-back rocker. It was her latest purchase and one she kept patting herself on the back for buying the moment she saw it at a recent arts and crafts festival she'd visited in a neighboring town. The wood was smooth and a golden brown in color, carved by an artisan's hand with skill and love. At least that's what she told herself. The artisan had offered it for sale but left no personal information about him or herself. The shop seller was just as reticent when it came to passing anything along to her as they loaded up her purchase. Once home, she had added the colorful cushion to the seat and it became her favorite spot for the early morning coffee she enjoyed as she began her day with the rising of the sun.

"Well, Peanut," she said to the large orange tabby cat that lounged in its usual place on the cushioned bench that sat in the corner of the porch, not far from Tori's usual rocking chair. The pair of them had their morning routine and their evening routine, as established over the years together. "You're in charge. I must get moving early this morning if I want to catch that worm," she said with a grin and a quick scratch behind a furry ear.

Driving along the tree-lined street that would wind its

way toward the outskirts of the town toward Lockwood Ranch, she pushed a button and allowed the sunroof to slide open, the morning air fresh and welcoming to her spirit. Drawing in a deep breath, she felt it was going to be a good day. She would explain to Caden Lockwood her vision for the warm springs on his ranch and how it would benefit so many of the townspeople, he would see the logic, and all would be fine. And he would understand why she hadn't simply waited until one of his assistants got back with a suitable time for an appointment with him. They had put her off one too many times already. *Take the bull by the horns.* That had become her motto, handed down from her grandmother, and she couldn't agree more. Caleb had to be a reasonable man, a smart man, to be in control of such an empire. They would have a business discussion. She had a positive feeling about it.

That positive feeling soon evaporated at the appearance of three cowboys on horseback standing just inside the double gates. She pushed the button and lowered her window, a smile ready on her face. Finally, one cowboy moved his horse closer to where she wouldn't have to speak so loudly to announce herself. He was an older gentleman, skin like weathered leather, and dressed in pure cowboy: spurs, chaps, hat—a hat that looked like it might have seen better days a decade or so ago. She had to give him props for that grayed handlebar moustache. He was straight from central casting for the next western film.

He tipped a finger to the brim of his hat and said in a slow drawl, "Howdy, ma'am. Are you in need of directions? Maybe lost?"

"Thank you, but no. I am in search, however, of Mr. Cade Lockwood. I'm mayor of Destiny's River, and if you would be so good as to point me in…" She didn't get to finish. A second horse moved forward to rest beside the other cowboy, and the rider was younger. He didn't have a welcoming smile. In fact, he didn't have a smile of any kind.

The first cowboy retreated. That left Tori to face the man seated on a very large black animal who looked like his unwelcome demeanor might match that of his rider. Did they practice that imperious gaze together? Again, she attempted her smile, but that was as far as she got.

"Once again, *Ms. Mayor*—" and the way he said those words did not bode well for them becoming friends "—you ignored instructions to apply for an appointment before coming onto my land. That might be how you do things in town, but not out here."

My land. The words caught and stuck in her brain. So, this was the almighty, powerful Caden Lockwood. *Just great.* And he had just made it abundantly clear that they were not destined to become friends anytime soon. Well, she had come too far and waited too long to let one moment go by before he threw her off his precious land.

Tori opened her door and stepped out, preferring to think better on her feet. Unfortunately, he seemed even taller than before for some reason. She raised her hand to help shield her eyes from the glare of the sun that was not in a most advantageous spot behind his shoulder. And it was a broad shoulder. And if she were not trying her best to hold her ground and patience, she might have taken in the fact that he was one of those cowboys women would enjoy staring at in awe as they passed by on the streets of town. But she was not here to ogle like a silly female. She was here on important business.

"No one invited you to step onto my ranch. In case you need it put any plainer, trespassing is an offense where we can employ force under our Texas laws. You need to get back inside your vehicle and head back to where you belong. My men and I have work to do."

"And so do I," she rounded back on him. "I have tried to obtain an appointment. I have been put off for almost a month now. I am just as busy in my office, I can assure you. But I represent Destiny's River, and the matter I need to speak with you about can wait no longer. Since you are here and I am here, I see no reason why we can't discuss the issue right now if need be. I won't take up your time any more than necessary, and then I'll be on my way."

"You already have taken up too much of my time this morning." He nodded at the third cowboy. He and his horse moved toward the panel next to the gate.

"I suggest you back your car out while you can. The gates are slow, but they can pack a punch. Nice chatting, Ms. Mayor. You have a good day." With that, minus a smile, he turned his mount and the pair of them left her in the dust…literally. The second cowboy followed in his wake. The third sat with solemn face, but his hand reached for the buttons inside the panel he had opened. She got the message.

Once inside the vehicle, she reversed and then wished she had her own cloud of dust on the highway she could kick up to punctuate her departure. Never had she been dismissed in such a rude manner. Well, he had another think coming if he thought she was some weak-minded female easily scared off once a male had put her in her place. She shook her head. If he wanted to play the game that way, then so be it. But waving a white flag in surrender on something so important as the warm springs was not in her DNA.

She saw how much people in and around their community could benefit by having access to those springs for health and rehabilitation issues. She wasn't asking for the keys to his kingdom. Just simple access to something that was merely sitting there and could mean so much to so many. Tori would regroup. Cade Lockwood hadn't seen the last of her.

Chapter Two

"YOU LOOK MIGHTY determined today. All done up in your suit and all," Minnie Smith noted as she finished the last of the breakfast buffet in the dining area on the back sun porch for the guests in the four small cottages at the back of the property, which all had porches with rockers overlooking the large flower garden and fountain. Tori had coaxed her into remaining at the Primrose Inn after Tori had finally been able to make the down payment and take it over from Addie Sims. Minnie was a feisty housekeeper/major domo around the inn, and she enabled Tori to venture out into the community and eventually run for office.

And Tori had definitely jumped off the end of the short pier into deep water. Running for mayor on the slogan of "Destiny's River…a future for everyone," she had simply embraced the country town that had embraced her and an orphan cat long ago. It was home, and she would make sure care was taken where needed for anyone who called it theirs.

"I have some meetings today. And I do believe my 'power' suit is called for." She laughed. The truth was she liked the newest purchase for her wardrobe. The navy jacket with thin white pinstripes, tailored slacks of the same material was given a flash of color by the bright scarlet silk blouse with its scarf tied casually and secured on her shoulder by a small gold ladybug pin her siblings had given to her when she began her term as mayor.

It was going to be a good start to the week. She could feel it. She gathered her scarlet shoulder bag and material for the office and with a last wave was on her way.

☆

AND THAT THOUGHT lasted within her mind all of fifteen minutes as she drove around the town square, found her reserved parking spot and then came to a screeching halt just in time to narrowly miss the bumper of the huge black truck that sat in her parking space…clearly marked with a sign that specified it was *Reserved for the Mayor*. The last time she checked, she was that mayor and that had been her parking space for the last six months, since her election. Everyone in town knew that.

Therefore, the lawbreaker must be from out of town. Spying another spot across the street, Tori pulled around and slid her small blue SUV into the parking place. Her door might have had an extra hard push as she put her hip into closing it with exasperation fueling her. Her arms full of the city maps and tax books she had taken home to study the evening before, she balanced them, her traveler's mug of coffee, and shoulder bag as she waited for clearance at the streetlight to cross the two lanes of traffic and head up the steps leading into the side door of the courthouse. Usually she would stop and admire the newly planted pecan trees sprinkled across the lawns, or the green squares of grass that the Ladies Garden Guild had planted to beautify the town's square, but she needed to stop into the sheriff's office before she went upstairs to her own.

"Morning, Ms. Mayor," came the greeting from the uniformed deputy behind the long counter as she stepped through the open doorway from the wide hall. Then he dropped his pen and hurried to come through the swinging gate that separated the reception area from the desks and other workers. "Here, let me help you out there." His arms were already taking the maps and the heavy books from her.

"Thanks, Monty, I appreciate it. I hadn't planned to stop here but I do have some business with the sheriff. Is he in and available?"

"That depends. Is it my sweet sister or the mayor of our fair town who is asking to see me?" The tall, uniformed figure nodded at his deputy standing with her items in his arms. "Monty, why don't you deliver those up to the mayor's office?"

"Yes, sir, on my way." He left the pair.

"Thank you, Monty," she called over her shoulder at his retreating back. "I owe you a milkshake over at Tillie's."

"Anytime, Ms. Mayor," he called out from the hallway.

"He's such a nice young man," she commented to the man standing in front of her, his arms crossed against his chest, waiting. "He'd be perfect for Reverend Lowry's daughter, Jennifer."

"So, this is you stopping in and giving me an update on your latest attempts as the quasi-town-matchmaker?"

"No, brother dear. This is *me*, a concerned citizen of this town, making a complaint to the sheriff. There is evidently a visitor to our fair county who doesn't know how to read signs. I almost collided with this hulking big truck parked illegally in my parking space out front. I think you need to have a deputy cite him or her."

"I see. Well, I shall certainly see that one of my deputies, one who is charged with making the rounds of the parking outside the courthouse, finds out about this interloper who had the audacity to displace our favorite city official from her rightful place."

Her hands went to her hips and she gave him her familiar big sister *look*...which spoke volumes without many words needed. "Look, little brother, you may have a shiny badge on your chest, but just remember whose dinner table you grace more often than not for home-cooked meals. That know-it-all grin can just starve if you get smart with me."

His hands went into the air to establish the fact he was giving in to an apology. "This department would never want to be accused of any complaint being made light of. We'll handle it with our utmost diligence."

"I am leaving it in your competent hands then." She smiled up at him. "It's meat loaf night, so don't be late." She turned and headed out the door. Another smile crossed her mind as she thought about how the lawbreaker in her parking space would soon get a special lesson.

"There you are," came the usual greeting from the older man seated behind the oak desk in the middle of the room, with its row of matching chairs rimming the two side walls. Wallace Samuels was the gatekeeper to her office. No one saw the mayor without being on his list. He guarded her time and he guarded her as well. It was a mixture of the benevolent uncle, the overprotective father, and the pit bull persona of an office manager that made it all hum with efficiency and she was forever grateful each day to be blessed with the man. If there was one word that was banned from everyone's vocabulary in the entire building, it would be *retirement.* He had retired once before in the previous administration. But he had come out of retirement in order to 'save the day' and bring order from the chaos left by his predecessor in the position. He was the epitome of country welcome guarding a steel streak underneath the friendly demeanor. He was her treasure, barometer of the day, and trusted advisor.

Wallace shared the large office space with two smaller desks in the back corners. Two office assistants, Gina and Dorothea, were his backups and handled other areas of the mayor's office and city business.

"Here I am." She nodded, continually moving even as she passed his desk and he handed over the stack of open mail that required her attention that morning, and any phone messages on their corresponding-colored paper indicating importance from the high priority of lime green to sunny yellow meaning it could be handled sometime that day, and the pale blue for maybe this week. He stood and followed her inside her office in his normal routine, ready to go over the daily calendar that he held in his hand. Gina would handle the outer office.

"Monty indicated you were in the sheriff's office and all the items you took home last night are on the sideboard behind you. I won't mention the fact again that homework is a bad habit to get into."

"And I thank you for not mentioning that" she said as

she began looking through the messages. "Seems we have someone who doesn't understand that a sign might keep one from getting a ticket for parking in the wrong space. But the sheriff's wonderful deputies will handle it all quite well."

Her smile slowly died away as she read and then reread the brief missive on the top of the messages…highlighted by being on lime-green paper.

"There is *that*," he commented as he settled into a chair in front of her desk.

"What is this?" she asked, the sticky green note wiggling on the tips of her two fingers as she held up the offending paper.

"Well, that would be a message from Mr. Caden Wright Lockwood. He stated that since the mayor kept later hours in the morning, he would just leave a phone message instead of wasting his valuable time in returning. He was here at eight a.m. on the dot this morning, at the office door when I opened it. When I told him you had not come into the office yet, he stood over me and dictated the message so I would get his wording correct. His words not mine. I will add that his presence made quite the impression on Gina and Dorothea."

"You mean by being an insufferable bore with an overstated sense of self-importance?"

"I believe they stated it in different words…such as 'drop-dead gorgeous'—that was Gina's comment—and 'a man's man but a woman's dreamboat' from Dorothea. He did give them rather nice smiles before he left. But I suppose he might be considered by some as full of himself."

"He is conceited," she corrected.

"He presents himself well. And he is somewhat of a huge rodeo star."

"A has-been showoff," she amended.

"Seems very determined to discuss a matter of importance with you."

"He can take a number, make an appointment like everyone else. He is not above anyone else in importance who comes to this office."

"I don't recall him being in this office since last year before the elections. He came in to speak to the former mayor for about five minutes."

"Yet, he lost the write-in election to me. That's what a person gets who doesn't invest his time in the community but simply sends emails to his minions. And then thinks he can expect to know what is best for this community. If he can't invest his time, then he can take his money and ego elsewhere."

"Now that's a shame," came a low drawl from the doorway, causing their heads to swivel up and around in its direction. The tall figure lounged against one shoulder in the open doorframe. "I was going to make a large donation to the city park renovation…since you haven't been very adept at pulling in donations. Maybe complete the campaign for you so that the youngsters might get to enjoy it sooner than later."

"Mayor Parker," Wallace said, getting to his feet and smiling at the newcomer. "May I introduce you to Mr. Cade Lockwood."

"I think she knows who I am." The rancher smiled in return. The Stetson he had held between the fingers of one hand slowly went back into its place on his head. His gaze went straight to hers. "And she knows where to find me if she wants to do the city's business."

Chapter Three

"WELL," WALLACE BEGAN, clearing his throat. The doorway stood empty.

"*Well, indeed.* He is all of what I said and more."

"I hate that he might have heard what we said. That was most unprofessional of this office. I will of course render apologies on our behalf."

"No, you will not. He should not have stepped past the ladies outside without an appointment or one of them stepping in to see if we could be disturbed. There are manners and rules and we do not apologize to someone who shows up uninvited and proceeds to issue his own orders or make hints of bribery."

"My. *My*, you certainly have taken a disliking to the man. Did something happen between the two of you that I don't know about?"

"Nothing has happened between us except when I tried to pay him a visit at his ranch three days ago, to introduce myself and be professional in thanking him for running a good election campaign and all, and then stating I wanted to discuss the possibility of his going along with a proposed plan that would allow for the city to benefit by access to the thermal pools on his property, he told me...no, and basically threatened me with trespassing. He acted like I was no better than any other politician who came with hat in hand wanting something from his family for nothing. And then he rode off on his high horse…literally."

"Quite an inauspicious beginning to say the least. I can see how things might have gotten off on the wrong footing. But perhaps…" Wallace did not get to finish the thought.

"No perhaps about it, Wallace. If he chooses to donate because it is a worthy cause, then he knows how to reach the Park Committee and make his donation through the proper channels. Let's set the mail aside while I make a couple of phone calls. Then we can continue."

"Will do." He shut the door behind him.

The nerve of the man! And so full of himself and his importance. What did he think she would do? Fall at his feet and thank him for his generosity and offer to hold a parade in his honor? He was as obstinate as she remembered. And he was so full of his charming self…she could well imagine how he had poured it on for Gina and Dorothea. Cade Lockwood was the golden boy of the Lockwood family…who all looked as though they were molded to be gorgeous and wealthy and above everyone else. How many photos had she seen of the man when she began to wade through the ton of materials that her team had gathered on her then opponent in the race for mayor? *Golden boy indeed.* Gorgeous…well those dark blue bedroom eyes as she had read described over and over ad nauseum might pause the heartbeats of most women, but she was certainly not one of them. True, she might have had to regroup her wits when he'd ridden up on his black horse the first time they met, the cowboy of the year in five rodeo events year after year, inducted last year into the hall of fame, and worth millions in family wealth and ranching. The list went on and on, but thankfully she had seen the true man behind the myth in their brief meeting and she was not a fan. Those types left her cold…and very irritated.

Luckily, the rest of the day went along as expected and she had to rush from the tax meeting well after six to get home and put the evening meal on the table. The back door opened as she was pulling the apple pie from the oven.

"Perfect timing," she remarked, and turned to set the pie on the cabinet. Then things went wrong. The person standing in the doorway was the apparition from her office…Cade Lockwood. The potholder slipped a bit in her loosened hold due to the unexpected shock and the hot pan's edge caught her off-guard and she felt the dessert leave her grasp. Her brother stepped inside right after Cade and couldn't move fast enough to do anything. Cade didn't move to save the dessert. His grip took hold of her wrist and turned her toward the sink. Cold water began running from the tap.

"Does anyone know where a first aid kit is?" His voice was calm and his brain clearly hadn't short-circuited.

"Here, under the sink," Matt spoke up, opening the cabinet underneath and coming up with the blue box.

"Burn cream?" Cade reached his free hand out to receive it from the sheriff. Matt placed it in his hand. "There's gauze, too."

"She might just need the cream and some air around it right now. It's pink but doesn't look worse than a side graze that shocked her."

She? Why had *she* become a bystander in the whole scene? And yes, it hurt like hell. But so did the grip he had on her wrist. A different sort of pain maybe…an irritation? Or just a shock that this man could so easily exert control over her body's sensitive spots. Maybe not wholly irritating. Aggravating mostly…that she would note it in the midst of all that was going on.

"I didn't know that you had an M. D. behind your name? I trust I don't need to worry about malpractice after your diagnosis?"

Those eyes cut over to hers. She hadn't noted the two deep grooves that appeared beside a very strong-looking mouth that half curled into almost a smile. But there was an imperfection, and she noted it…out loud before she could help it.

"Did someone break your nose for you? It isn't straight." As soon as she'd spoken, she wanted to die of embarrassment.

There went the rest of the smile, and it was blinding up as close as they were to each other. "No, *someone* didn't. More like somet*hings*…two different bulls that did that rearrangement for me. Some people think it lends character to me. What do you think, Ms. Mayor?"

"I always thought character was more an inside, unseen trait that people either have or not in their makeup."

"Touché," he whispered, accompanied by an almost imperceptible quick wink. So much so, she might have just imagined it. But she didn't think so.

"Excuse me, but if you let go of her wrist, we might get to have dinner at some point. We'll need another place set at the table, too." Matthew's comment was dry, and humor was just below the surface, but still dancing in his eyes as he watched the exchange.

Cade stepped away. But then he grabbed the roll of paper towels and began helping Matt clean up the remains of the damaged pie from the floor. It soon ended up in the trash can and the floor was cleaned.

"Sorry, I didn't warn you we were on the way. Or that I was bringing by news of the culprit who parked in your space this morning."

Tori busied herself setting an extra place and trying to gain control of her thoughts with the advent of Cade Lockwood in her kitchen after the way the day had begun. She was in for another surprise as they took their places at the dining table set into the alcove of the bright, airy kitchen.

"Well, if I had known, I would have had the table in the dining room set for a guest to join us. Since we usually eat here in the kitchen when it is just Matt and me and my niece—his daughter—pardon us being so casual." She sounded stiff even to her own thinking.

"Eating in the kitchen is the best place. That's how it was at our house while we were all at home, growing up. I still eat there myself. But I'm sorry about just barging in this evening."

"Well, I didn't give you much choice." Matt grinned, helping himself to the mashed potatoes. "I couldn't leave a prisoner to languish on jail food when we always have so much. Could I, sis? And this is killing two birds with one stone. I needed to see if you, the complainant, wanted me to hold the offender…that's this man sitting here with us…in contempt and have me pursue that with the court in the morning? The judge had already left the building."

"Am I missing something?" Tori was baffled. "What are you talking about, Matt?"

"Well, this morning you ordered me to do my duty and take care of the...how did you put it...the uneducated person who had no idea of how to read a sign and probably needed to have its importance explained to them like a child? Well, funny thing is that the person driving that monstrosity of a truck, as you called it, turned out to be Cade here. And he was in a hurry and just didn't pay the sign much mind, but it seemed he had to waste some time waiting on the person he had come to see and when he got back...well he found that little pink note that we officers like to leave on cars from time to time. So, I thought I would kill two birds with one stone...bring him along to get the complainant's decision on charges and enjoy some great food at the same time. Smart thinking on my part...wouldn't you agree, Mayor?"

She would agree to the fact her brother would be owed a payback big time in the near future. Whatever he thought his smart thinking was, it was a big mistake in her book.

Tori's gaze moved to the man sitting quietly watching the exchange between the two of them. Somehow, she had the feeling he had a large part to play in getting Matt to issue such an invitation. What was he up to?

"Interesting interpretation of the law," was her comment. She passed the basket of rolls to their guest.

"I thought so." Matt grinned, next taking the basket and helping himself. "Cade, these rolls are a whole food group in themselves. Take another." And the guest/defendant did just that.

For the next few minutes, eating was the order of the day. Tori was grateful for that. And she had already made a mental note to discuss a certain topic with her brother once they had an alone moment. Such as checking in with the hostess before surprising her with a dinner guest.

"That was just what I needed." Matt grinned again while rubbing his very full stomach. "I'll have to take that slice of pecan pie, or two, with me for a bedtime snack. How about you, Cade?"

"Would that be one of those pies that Tillie has over at the café? It looks a lot like one of them and they are indeed tasty. Tillie always has the best pies of anyone in town."

"Really? You think so? The best pies in town?" Tori was pleased that Cade was so easy to draw into her trap. She actually smiled at the man. Which drew a quizzical look from him in return. But he took the next step blindly.

"Sorry if that might bruise the ego, Mayor. But I know you wouldn't disagree that one of Tillie's pies is hard to beat."

"I wouldn't disagree at all. I'm pleased to hear you say so. I shall certainly take the compliment."

Cade looked confused. And Matt couldn't leave well enough alone any longer. His hand landed a pat on Cade's shoulder. "Hate to see a man fall so easily into my dear sister's trap. But that isn't Tillie's pie on your plate. In fact, each time you eat a pie at the café...you are eating a pie baked right here in this kitchen. The baker is sending you one of her *gotcha* smiles at the moment."

The light dawned across the rancher's face. "*You* did this?"

"Indeed. I did do that pie and all those others that you just proclaimed the best ever. It's a little hobby of mine, you might say. So now, when you go into Tillie's and order that slab of pie, you will think of me. Isn't that nice?" Her feigned sweet smile was perfect...in her judgment. The look in his narrowed gaze told her that he might not agree on that point. Matt pushed out of his chair and broke the moment.

"I've got to finish up a thing or two at the office and then want to check on Jillie at the sleepover at Janie Wilcox's house...covertly of course. Heaven help me if she catches her dad doing such a thing." He grinned and shrugged. "But then, I can't help it if a report came in and I just happened to have a call in the same block...across the street even."

"Always nice to see that devious streak is still there...even as you grow old." Tori stood and gave him a hug.

"I'm beginning to see a definite family resemblance in the both of you," Cade said, shaking his head as he joined the pair at the back door.

"We'll take that as a compliment," Matt said, taking his hat from the hat rack beside the door and pulling it down upon his head. Cade did likewise.

"So, what's the decision, Miss Plaintiff? I was about to forget the business that brought us here."

"I was wondering about that. Glad to see you remembered your duty, Sheriff," Tori responded, with a glance at the tall cowboy standing in silent regard of her. The girls in the office were wrong was the sudden thought that took over her brain. Those eyes were a deep sapphire blue...not just a dark blue as they opined. *And snap out of it!* The color of his eyes made no difference in the matter.

"A firm warning will do…*this time.* So, you can cut him loose, Sheriff. I trust he has learned a valuable lesson. And knows that an appointment is always the best idea…unless one has tried that and gotten nowhere." He wasn't going to catch her out so easily. "Do give my favorite niece a hug and kiss for me when she gets home."

Cade gave a slow smile that had the oddest effect on her coherent thought process. "Indeed, I have, Sheriff. I have seen a whole other side of our mayor this evening. And garnered some interesting information. I do appreciate the mercy you showed this lawbreaker this evening."

"And on that note, we won't push our luck any further. See you tomorrow, sis. Lock up tight." And the two men left her to do just that.

Chapter Four

TORI WISHED SHE had reconsidered and taken a second pill for her headache before she left the house that morning. She hadn't slept much, tossing and turning. Finally, she had given in and gotten up before the alarm sounded the usual six a.m. morning wakeup. It was a sluggish start to an already full day ahead of meetings, a ribbon cutting on the new dry cleaners in town, a working lunch with the very busy event planning group, and the list went on and on in her brain. The throbbing at her temple had arrived about the same time as the departure of the uninvited dinner guest the previous evening.

What was it about the man that just seemed to tilt her mood in the opposite direction from what it should be? Granted, he was somewhat full of himself—*somewhat*? Make that *a lot full* of himself—and wasn't hesitant in stating his opinions regardless of what others might be thinking. He had a knack for taking whatever position on a given subject that was in direct opposition to hers. Had his losing to her, a mere female, been that much of an irritant to his plans? He wasn't even planning to run, she was told, until she showed up as the only candidate. A spoiled cowboy with an ego too big for his Stetson was not her problem. He agreed that he had learned a lesson last evening and that was that. But somehow she would have to see proof of that one.

The brakes worked quite well as her foot stomped on them to the floorboard. Her front fender could be barely an inch from the fender belonging to an all-too-familiar big black truck...one that was parked dead center in *her* reserved parking space...*again*! Was the man that insane? Or just that much of an ego-maniacal fool? Did he think she was bluffing? That a smile over the dinner table would sway her opinion? Well, she would end this *right now*. Jerking her phone from her bag, she hit a number that was on speed dial. Her instructions were short and sweet and delivered with a gleeful feeling that seemed to have pushed aside her headache. Hanging up, she circled the courthouse and found a space on the opposite side, directly across from Tillie's Café. And her smile became even more pronounced as she drew the strap of her briefcase over her shoulder and in determined steps headed toward the café upon catching sight of someone she needed to share the news of the day with.

The bell over the doorway tingled its greeting along with the woman's verbal one as she stepped inside the busy café, the morning crowd busy with breakfasts and pots of fresh coffee.

"Hi, Tillie," she returned the greeting of the waitress behind the counter.

"Hiya, Mayor Parker. I bet you want your usual?"

"Not today. Just needing to say a quick word to that gentleman right over there. Thanks anyway." And she headed toward the man seated with his back to her, the person she recognized from across the street as he was seated almost dead center in front of the plate glass window of the eating establishment. There were two other men seated with him and they caught sight of her first and voiced their welcome.

"Well hello, Tori. Would you care to join us?" That came from Donald Mayes, the president of the largest bank in town. And Steven Haygood, the chairman of the local hospital added his invitation as well. Both men stood in the way of well-mannered country-born gentlemen reared by country mothers who demanded no less from their family males.

"Thanks, but not today, gentlemen. Please do sit and finish your food. I just thought I would stop in and say hello and hope you all have a good day today…especially Mr. Lockwood here."

Cade was clearly surprised by her appearance and more so by her words. "Well, that is very hospitable of you, Ms. Mayor. You seem to be having a good morning already."

"Oh, I am. I always feel so good when a wrong can be righted and it can teach a lesson at the same time."

His gaze narrowed on her. "And what wrong has been righted that has given you so much pleasure this morning?"

"Well, I think it only gives a positive reinforcement to our citizens when they see the laws of our town being upheld…no matter who it might involve. Wouldn't you agree?"

"Just what laws are being upheld?"

"Say, Cade," one of his fellow diners spoke up at that time, "that looks a lot like your truck that Davy Bales has on the back of his wrecker. But surely it couldn't be, I guess."

Cade's gaze left her and went to the window, and he did not quite react the way she had played out in her brain. He watched in silence. No immediate reaction. Then he took another sip from his coffee mug. Only after he had wiped his hands on his napkin and then folded it beside his plate, did his gaze return to hers.

"I can see what has made you so happy this morning. And I am pleased I was able to provide a reason for that. I was under the impression from a previous conversation you had with your brother last night that you would be later in the day after the ribbon cutting and a couple of meetings."

"Yes, well my schedule tends to be fluid on many days. A mayor must be flexible. And speaking of meetings, I'm going to be late if I don't rush away now." She gave a bright smile to his breakfast companions. "It was good to see all of you and do have a wonderful day."

"That includes myself as well?" He had to bring her attention to him again. She obliged.

"Why of course it does. It goes without saying what sort of day I would wish for you, too."

She turned and made her exit but not before she caught the glint in those eyes. A bit of fire? A hint of warning? *Too bad.* He wasn't going to spoil her mood. He would be busy the rest of his morning at the local tow lot reclaiming his truck. And she was humming as she crossed the street and moved her vehicle back into its rightfully reserved place. *Take that, Cade Lockwood.*

"You didn't. You wouldn't." The words were repeated once more by her brother as he sought to remain calm as he stood in the center of her office a few minutes later. "What made you do such a childish thing to a member of this community? You could have called me, and he would have gotten a ticket he would have to pay to the county. But nothing near what he will have to pay to reclaim his truck."

"And it will reinforce the fact that he needs to heed the laws of our town the same as anyone else. A *warning* clearly did little good. And the free meal he got out of it did nothing to sway his civic mindedness. Perhaps this lesson will be the one that makes the difference."

"Well, I would say that the afternoon meeting today hasn't an ice cube's chance in a boiling pot of being amicable and having him change his mind about access to the hot springs on his land. Thanks a lot, Ms. Mayor. You just remember that you did this to yourself…to all of us."

"Don't be so dramatic, Matthew. Of course, he won't change his mind about allowing access to those springs. He has made that abundantly clear. He is stubborn and selfish and cold-hearted and…"

"And standing right here." That effectively silenced the two people already in the room.

"And where is Wallace? How did you get by him a second time?"

"Your guard dog is nowhere in sight. One of the lovely ladies in the outer office allowed me to come right in. In the future, maybe you should practice closing your door when you want a private conversation."

"Maybe you should make an appointment before you even come to this office. Don't just drop in…uninvited."

"And maybe I hear my name being called downstairs," Matt said moving toward the open doorway as Cade stepped inside and out of his way. "Good luck."

"Who are you wishing good luck to?" Tori challenged.

Matt didn't miss a step but kept moving. "*Both* of you need it. Don't be late to the meeting."

"I have a meeting to prepare for," she said. That was a clear cue for him to leave.

"I have the same meeting."

Tori paused in shuffling her paperwork from one spot on her desk to another…a nervous habit that had seemed to develop with these unannounced visits from Cade Lockwood. "Since when have you started taking an interest in our meetings? You've always stayed away in the past." *What was he up to?*

"Since I was asked…very nicely, I might add…by the chairperson of the Future Development Task Force. You might take a page from her book."

"Shouldn't you be someplace else? Maybe at the tow yard?"

"Ah, yes. I have paid the fine and the truck is now in visitors parking. All nice and legal."

"That's refreshing. Glad to be of help in reminding you to follow posted warnings."

The sound of a clearing throat interrupted whatever else she might have added. Wallace stood in the doorway, an apologetic grimace on his face. "Sorry, Mayor, but I had stepped away to the post office. I thought the ladies could handle the office. And you have no appointments scheduled for this morning due to your council meeting."

"It's okay, Wallace. Mr. Lockwood was just leaving."

"Well," Cade drawled, sliding his hat onto his head. He nodded to both of them. "Guess that's my invite to leave. Have a good day, Wallace, and we'll see how yours goes in a little while…Mayor."

Was that a threat of some sort? The idea stayed with Tori as she gathered her folders and her copy of the agenda and soon slid into her seat beside the chair of the committee, Maggie Winston. She and Maggie had met through Addie Sims when the elder woman was selling Tori the Primrose Inn. Maggie had been born and raised in Destiny's River, left to go to college to get a law degree, and then came right back to her roots. Tori leaned over to whisper an aside to the woman before the meeting was called to order.

"Explain to me why Cade Lockwood had to receive a special invitation to this meeting. He seems to think you have more manners than I do so you've impressed him."

"Well, isn't that a nice compliment? And my question to you is why does that bother you?"

"Bother me? Did I say that?"

"Are you bothered because a gorgeous man complimented me and not you…or because he's here in this room, and his gaze has been on you since you sat down? Something has my friend all hot and bothered and I, for one, am pleased. Now, let's get this started." Her friend became the all-business legal brain and called the meeting to order.

Tori made a slow recon of the room. Besides the other five members of the committee, there were the handful of citizens that always made it their business to show up at each meeting, no matter the subject matter. They then would inform their fellow citizens of the goings-on at the café or other watering holes. Doing their 'duty' to keep an eye on their local officials or so they told themselves. Tori generally referred to them in her mind as the local 'busybody' society.

Then her gaze wavered as it was caught and held for longer on the person seated at the back of the room, looking as though he had settled in to watch something other than a formal committee meeting. And Maggie was right. Cade Lockwood had that semi-amused look on his face and he was watching her. Trying to catch her messing up? Well, he would have a long wait. She kept her attention on the speaker beside her. That worked right up until the time Maggie acknowledged the man and mentioned that he had asked to address the committee on a matter of importance. She was handing the floor over to him to speak his mind.

He unfolded his long length from the rigid chair and made a slow yet determined approach to the lectern on the table placed in front of the gallery and before the semi-circle bench area where the members sat.

"You contacted this committee wishing to speak on the matter before us, involving the request for usage of the hot springs located on the southern edge of the Lockwood Ranch. The city and county believe there could be positive benefits to the local inhabitants of our community. Yet you have thus far refused to enter into formal discussions with us as our representative, Mayor Parker, has attempted on three occasions to speak with you on this subject. We are still in the fact-finding stages of this matter. I understand you are here to speak with us today. You may have the floor, Mr. Lockwood."

"Thank you. I will be brief. The hot springs are on our land and have been as long as anyone can remember. It is the same with the natural springs that begin on the north side of our ranch property and flow into and form the river that bears the same name as this town was founded upon. Once the river leaves the boundaries of our land, it has always been for use as any of the other rivers in the state. The hot springs are situated on our property and the main pools are the same. The stream that results and travels away from the springs eventually flows into the river while still on our property.

"My grandfather's wish was always that these springs be kept in their natural state and safeguarded as private. It has been that way for generations and we maintain that it should stay that way for future generations. If the springs were open to the public, that would bring many other considerations into play...public access such as roads and sidewalks, adequate public restrooms. The flow of traffic on our private ranchlands would impact various other areas of our home and work. This would all require many and varied studies as to the feasibility and liabilities. I do not believe this city or county could handle the financial responsibilities involved here.

"And I respectfully request that this committee stand down from this plan and call off the mayor's office from continuing to bombard my office, my ranch hands, and myself with her requests and unannounced visits, disrupting my time and that of my employees. The answer is the same as it was thirty years ago, and three hours ago...we are not interested. The hot springs are on our property, and they are private."

There were a few moments of silence and then Maggie spoke up. "Thank you, Mr. Lockwood. It was always the intent of the committee, and our representative, Mayor

Parker, to open a dialogue where both sides could discuss the subject and bring any studies or other pertinent information to the table for examination. We do apologize for any unnecessary disruptions to your workday and employees. I am sure that was not the intent of the mayor."

Tori bit her tongue and managed to maintain what she hoped was an even expression on her face instead of wanting to indulge in throwing the stapler on the desk in front of her in the cowboy's direction to wipe that imperious look off his face. But she could bide her time.

"Certainly not the intention at all. But calls were unanswered, and meetings not scheduled. So, it was difficult to open discussions of any type, which made me take the time to move my schedule of the city's business to allow me to drive out to the Lockwood property to attempt to see and speak with Mr. Lockwood. In response to which, he ordered me off his land. I certainly will not attempt an in-person meeting again."

"Mr. Lockwood," Maggie began, "is it fair to say that most items such as the question of the hot springs and all their usage might entail to all parties involved, be thoroughly researched and all facts known to make an informed decision? I do believe there are volumes in our city library that detail the meetings and all that happened when the river was involved decades before. And those were wise people involved, including your grandfather and father, as I recall. There was even mention that you sat in on a few of those meetings during your holidays from college. I saw that noted, too. You would agree that all parties involved came to an agreement, and the people of our towns and county and beyond have benefited in many ways from such forethought."

"I would agree, yes."

"Mr. Lockwood, how much do you know about other locations and the benefits and or pitfalls from having provided hot springs for the use of their communities?"

"I admit that I know very little."

"Well. We applaud the fact that our mayor has spent many hours and weeks even on researching the pros and cons. Might you find time to do the same? Not starting from scratch as she had to do but perhaps you might be willing to take a day or two and allow us to share some of the findings in a neutral setting where hot springs have been a hot-button issue in the beginning and how they came to have a positive impact on their communities and all involved. You strike me as a businessman who does his research on a problem from both sides and manages to form an educated response, pro or con."

Maggie was good. She had just tossed a live grenade at the cocky cowboy. Tori clamped down on the grin that threatened.

"What does the chairwoman have in mind?"

"A joint fact-finding mission. At the county's expense of course. We will arrange for you and our mayor to tour one of three hot springs operations in our part of the country. See for yourself what we have in mind. After your research and consideration, return to this committee and whatever your decision after garnering the information for yourself, we will accept your final decision. I think that is a fair handling of such an important issue for this community...would you agree?"

"If all members of your committee agree that the answer would be final on the subject…then I am willing to agree…to this fact-finding mission. But perhaps the mayor might have a crowded schedule and would prefer to not participate?"

Her turn. A smile appeared on her face. "The mayor believes this a very important issue and will clear whatever is necessary on her schedule." *So, take that…the game is on.*

"Good," Maggie said, and others nodded agreement. "We will look forward to your report back to us, Mayor Parker, and to your decision, Mr. Lockwood. Next on the agenda."

Tori wasn't surprised the rancher excused himself, sweeping his hat onto his head as he headed for the exit. But he paused and turned…catching her gaze. And there was no mistaking the glint in his eyes…and then a slow wink that clearly sent the message straight to her…

Game on indeed.

Chapter Five

"I'M IMPRESSED. PUNCTUAL and you pack light." Cade could have added that she was also a female who didn't have a problem with getting up before the sun. But he didn't want to push his luck. So far, things had been 'pleasant.' But there was no guarantee that would last. Tori Parker stepped forward with her small suitcase in hand as he opened the back door of his truck. He moved to take the case from her but she sidestepped and lifted the case on her own and placed it inside. She did allow him to close the door as she stepped back.

Small victory. He went for double or nothing. Cade did a quick move and managed to reach around her, and his hand met hers on the door handle of the front passenger-side door. "I believe I got here first." He added a smile as she slowly released her hand with reluctance from the top of his. She stepped onto the running board and then up into the passenger's seat. He shut the door.

What is her problem? She's like a prickly pear cactus that fairly shouts: don't get too close. Cade climbed in and noted the way her gaze was taking in the interior of his truck.

"Sorry if the truck isn't your preference. I like to be prepared when traveling some of the mountain roads where we're headed. My Boy Scout upbringing I guess." That bit of humor fell flat as that blue gaze stayed steady on him for a moment or two.

"A Boy Scout," she finally responded. "Who would have guessed."

"Indeed. Well, daylight is burning. Let's get this excursion underway." The engine purred to life and they headed out of town.

The silence in the cab was notable. If she wanted silence then she could have it, was his plan. After a good twenty minutes of it, he was the one to wave the white flag.

"Only four hours and twenty minutes to go. Time flies."

"When you aren't having fun," she responded. Not what he would have expected…exactly. "One would think given all the gauges and gadgets that this truck is decked out with, you'd have a button to move us to warp speed."

He had to grin. Did she have a sense of humor locked inside that cool exterior? Granted that she wasn't bad on the eyes. If one liked reddish-gold hair that seemed to be worn in a perpetual ponytail at the back of her head, allowing a good length to hang over her shoulder. The side view highlighted the straight set of the jawline—more like the stubborn line of her jaw, he amended in his mind. A nose that might be described as pert…a bewitching upturn at the end which made him think of a witch from a television show on late-night fare.

The one item that caught attention most often, he would wager, were those eyes. Dark eyelashes framed them, and they only heightened the incredible azure blueness…the color of a lake he once backpacked to in the high country. That memory had popped into his brain the first time she'd faced him down on his property…right before he'd ordered her back into her car and off his land. Not the best of first meetings, he had to admit. The fact that she fitted into the prerequisite jeans quite nicely hadn't gone unnoticed. The oversized sweatshirts and blouses with jackets in the office were okay but he had to wonder why she might not step up her look once in a while. Of course, it was no concern to him.

"Warp speed? I can imagine that there might be some member of the city council in Destiny's River who could find reason to impound my truck next if I tried that."

"I had no idea you still harbored bad feelings about your truck being towed…even as it was an obvious violation of the law."

"No bad feelings here, Miz Mayor," he drawled. "I have always been a law-abiding citizen. I just never figured you for one who followed space movies."

"And why should you? We're virtual strangers. Even though you did express personal opinions when you ran against me for mayor."

"I believe that we kept our political differences to the issues."

"For the most part. But you did keep alluding to my not being a part of your community and such. Which is ridiculous since my brother has been the duly elected sheriff here for two terms now. And I have been in the community for over a decade…most of it as a business owner. One can be a good citizen and supporter of the place where they have roots. Mine might not be quite as deep as your family's, but then my ancestors weren't here to form the first community.

Even so we can still be invested in it."

"That you can. That is a fair statement. Your brother has been a fine sheriff and done a good number of positive things for the town and county. I agree I don't know that much about your little inn, but it seems to be a popular place and well thought of among others in the community."

"Exactly why did you agree to this *excursion*, as you call it?" She now gave him her full-force gaze that had a way of pinning you to the topic at hand whether you wanted to be there or not.

"I believe it was Maggie who gave it that name first."

"Don't be obtuse. You know what I mean. You complain about how busy you are, yet here you are...going to someplace I am certain you would not have on your radar ever and with me along...a thorn in your side. Did that clarify the question for you?"

"I remember that one of those campaign slogans of yours said something along the lines...plain talk and determination...and that does seem to sum you up. So why not see if that is really your stance or is this just some political grandstanding on your part? Others have tried to gain control of our land in one way or another, but this is certainly a different angle."

"I can assure you that this is no political angle, as you put it. And you would realize the positives involved here if your hat wasn't so tight on that big head of yours." She turned her attention to the window beside her, arms crossed in front of her, and a very determined set to the jaw visible.

Silence again. He would have come right back with a smart reply...usually. But he had an idea that would get him nowhere. And he needed to get through this little exercise in patience and then get back to the committee and tell them no way, no how, and discussion was closed for good. Then he and Miss Lady Mayor could go their separate ways.

But in the meantime, they needed to get along. What was her story anyway? Her brother was a nice enough guy. Reasonable and dedicated to the community. Caleb had tried to pull bits and pieces from his memory of the campaign materials, but that had been a while back. Maybe he would do his own brand of fact-finding this trip also. What made this obstinate woman tick?

"Okay. I think we need to bury the hatchet."

She turned and looked at him once again, a fine eyebrow raised in silent question.

"Bury the hatchet, you say? Bury it where?"

"You do have a sense of humor—I will give you that," he responded. "We agree to disagree…in an amicable way as we both keep our minds open over the next couple of days. Then we can have a calm discussion after all the facts are in. That's agreeable, isn't it?"

"We'll hold judgment on the 'calm' part of that statement for now. But, yes, after all, we all want what is best for the people of Destiny's River—*all of them*." She sent that point his way and he would allow her to have the last word. This time. Little did he know that their peace accord would soon be put to the test in more ways than one.

☆

"WE'RE GLAD THAT you folks will be staying with us," the

courteous manager greeted them once they arrived at their destination. “Glad to have you visit our springs and if you have any questions we can answer about our project here, we will be glad to do so.” Then he added, “There is just a minor change we have had to make in your earlier reservations. We had a bit of unexpected weather come in early yesterday…luckily it swept through and has given us better weather now. But it did do some damage to the units we had earlier placed you in. And it is really for the better. We have you in our Grandview Cabin. It’s an upgrade at no extra charge to you of course.”

“Didn’t we have two rooms before?” Tori chimed up when warning bells sounded in her brain.

“Yes, ma’am, and this cabin is one of our family cabins with two sleeping areas. It has a much nicer view of the mountains and it’s closer to the hot springs area.”

Tori caught the hint of amusement in Cade’s face before he took the keys and turned to the bags. He picked up both before she’d realized. She went to take hers and was met with a shake of his head. “You take a key and lead the way.” He nodded at one of the keys in his hand closest to her. She decided not to argue and headed in the direction the desk clerk indicated.

A few minutes later, they stood at the bottom of five steps that led upward to a porch surrounding a structure consisting of huge brown logs.

“An old log cabin.” The male tones were flat.

“A rustic, picturesque log cabin.” She corrected his depiction.

“Picturesque?” His gaze upon her was skeptical. “That

would be an exaggeration in anyone's book."

"Well, we aren't writing a book, nor are we here for the accommodations," she informed him. "We are here for the hot springs and time is wasting." Tori took determined steps upward. The porch was wide and to its credit there were two cane-back rockers and a porch swing. "Very inviting," she pointed out as she fit the key into the lock and the door creaked open on its hinges.

She looked at Cade who had joined her much slower on the porch.

"Ladies first," he said, waiting for her to step inside.

"Fine."

Once inside, he stepped around her and went in search of the two rooms. She remained in the center of the living room/kitchen area that formed a fair-sized main room. The furnishings matched the rest of the cabin: log-hewn walls, open crossbeams overhead, a wagon-wheel hanging light fixture with milk stone lanterns, wooden flooring with large throw rugs in Native American weave forming an oasis for the deep-seated cushioned couch and two overstuffed chairs with end tables and lamps in a horseshoe arrangement framing the stone fireplace that filled the wall floor to ceiling.

"Small issue, Miss Mayor," he announced, coming back into the living room.

"Why am I not surprised?"

"There are two sleeping areas."

"Yes, I believe I have heard that before. What's the problem?"

"Follow me." He turned and she was left to do just that.

She assumed the room was the master bedroom. The

four-poster bed, king-sized, was covered with a brilliantly colored, star-pattern quilted center. The frame was tall, and she was glad to see that a small step stool was beside the bed. There was a smaller fireplace in the corner of the room with another deep-seated chair, and a larger matching footstool in front of it.

"Very nice," she commented.

"Glad you think so," he said and his tone alerted her brain. "So where is the other bedroom?"

She headed toward the single door in the far wall. But he stopped her.

"That's not it. That is the bathroom." He walked over and flipped on a small lamp that illuminated an alcove…with a bunk bed tucked away in the corner. "This is the second bed area. Care to flip a coin?"

"I would say you've got to be kidding, but I'm afraid to hear the verification that you aren't."

"Nail on the head," he responded. "This could handle a family of four…if two of the party were midgets and, gauging from the size of the bunks, young children."

"And the desk clerk already verified this is the best they have now. So, I guess you'll have to check out the sofa and see if you can make do with that."

"*I'll* have to make do with the sofa? No discussion. *You* just decided."

Was he serious? He certainly looked serious. "Okay, here." She rummaged in her bag and came up with a quarter. "We'll flip for the big bed. Loser takes the bunks or the couch. And I'll even let you flip the coin and call it first. Heads or tails?"

"You're serious? You willing to gamble and lose the bed? Just forget it. I'll take the couch."

"Are you afraid to gamble? Thought you rodeo cowboys gambled every time you got on a wild animal. Or is that just television?"

He took the coin from her outstretched palm. "Okay. We'll toss for it. I call tails."

She smiled. "Appropriate in a variety of ways. I get heads—toss it."

And he did. And he lost.

"And that is that," she said. And while it was very difficult to not rub salt in the cowboy's possibly wounded pride, there were more important tasks ahead. They were here to win him over on the question of the springs. "I'll change into my other shoes and be ready to take a tour of the facilities in five minutes. You'll be ready?" She began to unpack her bag.

His reply was to grab his bag from the floor and retrace his steps into the living room. The door shut behind him with a little more decisiveness than expected. Which only made her smile more. The full-of-himself cowboy might learn a little attitude adjustment along with the facts on this trip.

He was waiting on the front porch of the cabin when she next saw him. He glanced at his watch. "Two minutes to spare."

"I am a strong believer in punctuality. It was ingrained in me from an early age."

"An early age?" He cast out the question. Perhaps fishing.

Tori smiled and headed down the steps to the path. "Can't waste the daylight. We'll begin with the lower pools and work our way to the top. Sound like a plan?"

He had to move it a bit to catch up with her determined steps. "Asking for my input?"

"Of course," she replied, not breaking stride. "You're a *no-nonsense* type of businessman…or so I've been led to believe. So wasting time would not be something you would want to do…correct? But if I'm going too fast for you, I can slow down."

"No need to slow down on my account. That's fine in business. In other areas I prefer to take things nice and slow, but that's *other* things."

Was that a pesky stone in the path that tripped her up? His hand shot out quick enough to lend a steadying grip on her elbow. She righted herself from the stumble and continued her stride. His hand went back to minding its own business. "Thanks, but I've got this."

"As always, it seems." The words were lowered, and she didn't have full control of her breathing at the moment to respond, so she let it slide. He could think whatever he liked. It was a stone in her path that made her unsteady, not anything he said or the ridiculous reaction it conjured up in her brain to whatever innuendo he might have alluded to. *Get a grip. You don't even like the arrogant rancher. You are not some groupie.*

"Here we are," she said, glad of another focus for her mind. The map in her hand corresponded to the information on the sign posted at the first hot springs. "You can read the information for yourself. This is a small pool set aside for smaller groups…individuals and couples…even parent and child as seems to be the case that we can see."

It was evident that a mother was trying to get a second, mostly reluctant little boy into the pool but he was having none of it. The other child was watching from a submerged seat against the far wall. Mom was pleading, then resorting to a more parental tone of authority, and ultimately attempting to bribe the child, who looked to be about seven in age, with promises of his favorite dessert and of watching a television show before bedtime. He was staunch in his refusal.

"Okay, which one of you youngsters is the best cannon-baller?" The question surprised all of them into silence, including Tori. All eyes were on Cade. "It takes a lot of practice to get it right. I bet it's you?" And he pointed at the younger child sitting quietly, eyes round with surprise. He shook his head quickly enough. "What's that?"

"You two don't know what a cannon ball is?"

The older boy spoke up. "I do!"

"Well, I doubt that since most cannon-ballers…really good ones…are always in the water working on bigger splashes. You don't even get into the water as far as I can tell. So, you can't be very good at it."

"I am, too. Watch me." And the child took his stance on the edge of the pool and did his tuck and hold in midair, and a splash erupted when he hit the water. The boy came up and quickly looked with triumph at Cade. "See?"

Cade made a show of serious consideration. "I don't know about that. It was a weak splash. You sure you've been practicing? I bet your mom and brother there might like to see how much better you can do…if you really want to be the best."

The boy was already climbing out and taking his stance again. "I'll show them."

"Then we'll leave you to it to get some practice. Practice will make you the best at whatever you do. Keep at it."

He met the grateful smile of the mother with one of his own and a knowing wink as the boy made good on another jump.

As they walked away, the sounds of more splashes could be heard.

"Who knew you had some child psychology mixed in with your knowledge of cattle? Very surprising. Unless you have a child or two I haven't heard about?" She ventured a glance in his direction as they walked toward the next pool.

"Not much psychology needed. I just had grandparents who knew how to raise kids. I learned by their example. And no to your other question...I have no kids."

"By design...you don't want any?"

"That's a personal question, isn't it, Mayor? Do I get to ask the same of you?"

"Pardon me. I overstepped."

"Ah...got personal for you. Well, I can share quite frankly that it isn't by design as you call it. I want kids...someday. If and when the right person comes along. So far, that has not happened."

"I see."

"Somehow, I doubt that you do see...but then we aren't destined to be buddies, so such sharing isn't really required. And that's more to your liking."

Tori stopped in her tracks and turned to face him. And maybe that wasn't the best of moves on her part. *Much too close…and too…personal.* And in an instant, she knew that he had been baiting her. It was a game to him.

"You are correct…no to the buddy idea. But there is fair play. You answered so I'll give you one back. I may not have the experience of observing great parenting, but I've seen enough bad parenting skills to know what not to do. Enjoy the compliment I gave you. Odds are there won't be that many of them."

Chapter Six

"THE NEXT TIME you come up with an idea like this…*don't*!" Maggie had called just as a rain cloud had ended their brief tour of the springs and opened a floodgate as they made it back to the porch of their cabin. They had both parted to find a change of clothes before thoughts of dinner could be discussed.

"Tori, are you on your best behavior? Remember, you can get more done with honey than vinegar."

Tori shook her head. "Maggie, this is business, and I don't think honey would go far with this man. Anyway, I have been pleasant."

"Pleasant…why does that not sound so pleasant?"

"He's stubborn. He's already made up his mind and this is going to turn out to be a waste of time."

"Has he said that?"

"Not in so many words, but I just don't think he's taking this seriously. It's a game of some sort."

"Then it's up to you to teach him some new rules of the game. You've fought long and hard for this idea to come to fruition and now you have him sort of captive so make the most of it. I would say use your charm but that might be asking too much."

"A *lot* too much. But I'm not giving up yet. It's pouring

rain right now, but once it passes, we'll get back on track. If this fails, it won't be because *I* didn't try."

"That's the spirit." Maggie agreed with a laugh. "That's the Tori we all know and believe in. Now go smother him with sweetness and all those facts packed in your head…*and smile*!"

"Smother him," Tori said aloud as she dropped the phone back onto the bed. "That might be more manageable than smiling at him."

"So, I shouldn't close my eyes tonight for fear of a pillow being dropped on me?"

She swung toward the doorway and the man in question stood looking around the edge of the slightly opened door.

"I *did* knock. But I guess you couldn't hear for the thunder and rain on the metal roof."

"Well, you should have knocked louder then…and waited for a response before just barging in. And you might work on looking more apologetic."

"Apologetic? You are asking a lot there, Miz Mayor."

"And my name is Tori. You may use that and drop all this Miss Mayor stuff."

"Tori," he tried it out. "And that would be short for?"

"Victoria. But few people call me that unless I'm in trouble and that is usually my family." Why had she shared that with this man?

"Tori does suit you…in most cases. But I'll keep an eye out for those situations where Victoria might be more appropriate."

She grimaced inside. Too much information shared. She knew better. But there was something about this man that seemed to keep her off her usual centered self. And that was just another irritant to chalk up to the cowboy.

"Was there some reason you're standing here talking to me?"

"Right. Yes, the rain is not letting up, so I took the liberty of calling over to the lodge and they're delivering food in one of their vehicles. And I've got a fire going in the fireplace out here to get the chill out. So don't worry about getting out in the weather again. Hope that's okay with you?"

"Sounds like you've handled everything, so I'll just finish up in here and be out in a minute."

He just nodded and closed the door.

Tori was hoping for a dining room with other people and now they would have to find conversation between only the two of them. The evening suddenly loomed ahead. But Maggie was right. This was the final chance to do something that would mean a lot to so many. Squaring her shoulders, she decided she would be up to the challenge.

☆

THE FOOD ARRIVED and Cade began arranging it on the small table he'd found by the back door and moved it closer so that it was a few feet from the fireplace. He added two chairs. He glanced at the candleholders on the mantelpiece, but quickly shook that thought away. This was not an intimate dinner between good friends. It was at best to be a stilted negotiation. The door creaked open behind him as he laid the last napkin on the table.

"I'm just about to set the food on the table," he tossed

over his shoulder while placing the last of the silverware. "I wasn't sure of a preference for you, so I got both beef and chicken fajita platters. It was that or…" He made the mistake of turning at that moment to speak directly at the woman who had entered. That's when his brain stalled on him.

Tori…or was it Victoria…had changed. Nothing too major but it was just enough. Fresh jeans topped with a nice figure-hugging deep blue sweater, the tiny pearl-white buttons of the front catching the firelight as she moved slowly into the room. But it had to be her hair that caught him off guard. Gone was the customary ponytail. A mass of hair fell over and below her shoulders, its rich sable-brown color caught the light in the softer golden streaks through it. There was a sudden itch in his fingers gripping the salad forks to feel its softness…test to see if it felt as it looked.

"Or?" Those blue eyes had grown even more blue as they watched him with a quizzical glint in them.

"Or…" *Snap to it, brain.*

"You said there was another choice you almost made?"

"Fish. It was fish."

"Good. I'm allergic to fish. So best we steer clear of visiting the ER tonight. Wouldn't want the constituents back home thinking you might have done it on purpose."

"Done it?"

Now she was looking at him far closer.

"Fed me something that is bad for me. Did something happen since our last conversation? Are you okay?"

"Yes. No…the food came, that's all. Trying to think if I ordered all we need." He stepped to pull her chair back, his brain kicking into gear.

And he had an answer to his previous thought as his fingers on the chair encountered strands of the thick hair on her shoulder. He jerked them back as if they were hot to the touch. The movement wasn't lost on her by the way she glanced up at him. He moved around the table and took his own chair. *It's just a simple business dinner. Get with it.*

The silence threatened to become deafening as they each tasted their food.

"The food is..."

"Didn't know if..."

They both stopped as soon as they spoke in unison.

"Ladies first," he said, gaining his faculties.

"I was about to say that the food is quite flavorful. A good choice for a rainy night."

"Thanks. And I was going to say I didn't know what you preferred to drink until I remembered you preferred iced tea that evening at your home. So, I did order unsweet but also ordered a lot of sugar in case you liked it sweet."

"That's thoughtful of you, thank you. I do love some tea with my sugar," she said with a grin at the joke she had made. "I'm a Texan who loves sweet tea."

"No apologies for that. So do I. Afraid I never quite got into the wine thing."

"Really? But there is a wine that has your ranch's branding on it...or did I dream that?"

"No dream. That would be my sister's part of the family business. Granddad left her a place down in the Hill Country and she took to wine making. Five years and it just might pay off for her."

"It's just you and your sister, correct? I've never met her."

"Correct. We are the last of the Lockwoods. Unless she gets busy and leaves her vineyards long enough to find a husband and procreate."

"And you leave your cows long enough to do the same? Sorry, that was personal."

"If I frowned, it's not at the question being personal. It's just something I don't put much store in happening."

"I would say that I see, but not really. You had a real rapport with that little boy earlier."

"Maybe I might adopt later on…or just be a favorite uncle and spoil them and make my sister pay for all her antics growing up…which I usually got blamed for."

"It's the marrying part that you don't seem keen on."

"Very astute of you…Tori. A person in my position, well I am aware that my bank account is catnip for many women. But I have seen some good marriages…even a great love story, but I've seen more bad than good. And now, I get to ask where are your husband and kids…or are you destined to move up the political ladder alone?"

"I don't know about the political ladder. I'm happy right where I am in Destiny's River. This is home. And if I can talk my other siblings into it and have them move nearby, then that will be perfect as far as I'm concerned. I won't be greedy and ask for more. Just a good place for those I love."

"And you work very hard for that…and for a lot of others. I've heard your praises sung often enough around the county. You seem to want to accomplish a lot. But there are some battles you will win…and some you won't. The question will be if you can handle that defeat when it comes."

"I'm not a stranger to disappointment or defeat. I'm not a dainty hothouse flower. I do know what is worth fighting for and what is not meant to be. And on that note, Mr. Lockwood, if you haven't realized it by now, I intend to fight like hell to get you to change your mind on the springs on your property. It means too much to too many and I intend to show you that tomorrow...given that old Texan saying...if God is willing and the creeks don't rise between us and the rest of the things here that you need to see. Thanks for this dinner. But this politician does have a job and a briefcase of paperwork I brought with me. I'll leave you to enjoy the fire."

She stood and he did the same. Time had gone faster than he thought it would. *Imagine that.* And he was sorry it had done so. "Would you like me to set a fire in the fireplace in your room?"

Tori smiled at him. It suited her. "Thanks, but if I want one later, I do know how to start it myself. And don' worry about disturbing me if you come in later and I'm asleep."

"Don't worry about me. I think I'll be just fine on that couch over here. It's longer than that bunk bed in there. This will do for me."

"There are extra blankets in the closet in there if you need them. I can get them for you."

He stopped her with her hand on the doorknob. "No thanks. I found a couple in the hall closet and pillows, too. You don't have to worry about me, Tori Parker. I'm one constituent of yours who knows how to take care of himself. One less for you to worry about."

"We'll see. Sleep well."

The shutting of the bedroom door made the room seem less warm…have less light in some way. Cade looked around. Nothing had really changed except she had left the room. And he was alone. Why should that make a difference? He had been okay with being alone with himself for a good number of years. One determined female with blue eyes wouldn't be changing that.

"Sleep well, yourself, Miss Mayor. You aren't changing this man's mind."

Would it have sounded better to his ears if he had stomped his foot as the period on the sentence? Because for the first time in a long time, there was something strangely resembling cautiousness in his display of optimism at winning out. Well, tomorrow the storm would have passed, the sun would be back, and he would feel like himself again. *Perspective.* That was it. He had something clouding his usual perspective. But tomorrow…clarity would be back, and she would see that she had lost this battle.

Chapter Seven

"GOOD MORNING! IT'S a beautiful day. Hope you like coffee without cream…they left it out of the sack. And I have two kinds of breakfast tacos…one with sausage and one with bacon. Which would you prefer?"

Was it the smell of the coffee or the food that had the man rising to a sitting position on the couch? He wasn't smiling though. Tori placed the cup of coffee in the hand he had freed from the blanket and the other was still empty.

"Bacon is in my left hand and sausage in the right," she said, making it easier for him.

He pointed to the right. She handed over the sausage taco in its foil wrapper.

"Okay then, looks like you might not be a morning person. So, finish up your breakfast and I'll just wait outside in one of those rockers with my food." She headed to the front door and then added, "Be sure and add your swimming trunks as the springs we're headed to this morning might do wonders for your morning disposition."

She had just finished the last of her taco when the door opened a few minutes later. Caleb was dressed in jeans and a long-sleeved red and gray flannel shirt. He looked good even with a day's growth of scruff on his cheeks. And that was something she didn't need to contemplate.

"Ready for our next adventure in your education? Or do you need another cup of coffee?"

"Are you always so cheerful in the early morning?"

"I try to be. A good cup of my coffee does wonders and my own rocking chair overlooking my own garden always helps. But there are mountains to see here from this porch and fresh air to breathe."

"I see."

"Oh! Look, isn't it incredible?" She had jumped up from the rocker and her gaze was on the driveway. He turned to see what had transformed her so quickly.

A herd of horses, all sizes and colors, was being herded quickly up the drive until they turned just before the cabin and were trotting by as if on display for her enjoyment. A couple of the cowboys riding along with them raised a hand in greeting and grinned at her enjoyment.

"Isn't this great? They're incredible. Horses are so beautiful." Cade was enjoying watching her watching them. It was a totally different side of her. Perhaps there were a lot more layers to this woman than met the eye.

"They're just saddle horses, probably bringing them down from the high-country pastures."

"I think they are all beautiful no matter what they are. I always wanted a horse growing up. I wanted to be adopted by people who had horses. That was what I kept telling the social worker." Then she stopped, her gaze remaining on the disappearing herd.

"You were adopted?"

She remained silent for a few moments. The excitement of earlier had disappeared when she finally turned back to him. "No. I was never chosen. And we are wasting the morning. I heard them say when I was picking up the tacos that there may be more storms heading our way after lunch so let's get moving." She grabbed the small bag that sat across from her on the side table and headed down the steps. He followed slowly.

It was clear that the mood had changed. Cade was mulling over the last few minutes and realized it had to do with his asking about adoption. He had no idea that there was obviously something in her family that she wasn't into sharing…at least not with him. Or was it just at the moment? He'd steer clear for the time being.

"This is a spring pool that I think you'll find interesting." Her words brought him back to the moment and he could see an older man and a younger one on one side of the pool. It was evident that the younger one was working with the man on some exercises for his legs. Across from them was another person with a little girl lying across her outstretched arms. Perhaps teaching the child to float? He followed Tori to one of the two benches that sat beside the pool. On the other bench was a woman and man intently watching the child's progress.

"Hello," Tori said, taking the empty bench seat. "Is it okay if we sit for a few minutes? We don't want to disturb you."

"Please do sit," the woman responded. "Our daughter is almost done with her therapy session. And she is so focused on the work that she tunes all else out."

"Therapy? This is one of three such pools, correct?"

"Yes, there are three. The rest of the pools are for families and tourists...the public. There is a limit placed on them of course and that is nice. It doesn't get crazy like some pools do. Many come just to relax. Others, like our daughter, use the hot springs as part of their physical therapy."

"And the therapists are on staff here?"

"No, actually," she responded. "They're on the staff of the local hospital and the doctors prescribe the treatments. Jessie, that's our daughter, was injured when a car crashed into her school bus waiting at a stop sign. That was three months ago."

"She's been working with a therapist in this pool that long?" Cade had his own question.

"Only for the last six weeks. After the crash, she had no use of her legs. We were afraid she might not regain it. But with a wonderful doctor and lots of therapy, she can actually take a couple of steps before she needs help now. The doctor thinks she'll be back walking again. We had almost lost hope when we started this, but it has been amazing for her. And there are others...such as that man over there, Mr. Gardner. He had a stroke, paralyzed along one side. But he has arm movement now and they are seeing improvement in his leg. This is a wonderful place."

"The pools are not just for pleasure and fun. That's interesting."

Tori smiled. "That is wonderful to hear. Thank you for sharing and we hope Jessie will continue to heal." They walked along the winding path. A gentle breeze had picked up. Sounds of laughter and conversations drifted in and out. The largest pool was at the highest point on the property with an unblemished view of the surrounding mountain range where snowfields were still in evidence on the highest slopes.

☆

TORI SAT THE bag on a table under an umbrella and took out the towels she had brought along from the cabin. She looked over at Cade. "You swimming in your clothes? I would advise against it."

Just business. Negotiating in a bathing suit…always a first time for everything. She wound her hair up in a coil and secured it at the top of her head with a clip she also took from the bag. As long as she kept busy, then the nerves that were playing just below the surface would be manageable. It wasn't as easy to keep her attention off the fact of the sound of Cade standing just a couple of feet away, a shirt being unbuttoned and landing on the table, the zipper sounding next. Maybe she should have just ended with lunch and a discussion in the dining room. Too late now.

"Last one in buys dinner," she called over her shoulder and then the next thing she knew she had a mouthful of spring water and was coming up for air. *So much for a graceful entrance into the pool.* But she had made the mistake of looking back at Cade, registering the site of rock-hard abs, broad shoulders with muscled arms and long legs that made her misjudge the distance to the second step down into the pool. So, it was really the man's fault. That made her feel better…for a moment.

"You okay? Need a hand?" The hand appeared in front of her as she clung to the side of the rock ledge.

She shook her head and waved the offer of help away. "No thanks. I'm fine. Not my most graceful entrance, but I did beat you into the water. I am thinking a juicy steak tonight…since you'll be buying."

She turned and swam away from him with strokes that were a lot more graceful. All was well for a few minutes. She made a show of doing laps all the while she was aware of Cade, treading water and then seeming to stop and lean against the opposite rock ledge, a thoughtful deep furrow creasing his brow as if pondering some deep subject. Maybe he was having second thoughts about his negative decision of allowing the private springs on his land to go public. At least a girl could hope for such a thing to happen. This was their last shot at what she considered a no-brainer. But the man was stubborn. And much too good-looking for his own good. She noted the way a handful of the ladies in lounge chairs around the pool had taken a sudden interest in him. Who wouldn't? She'd admit he was one fine male specimen. But she was sure he knew it, too. And she wasn't going to be another fawning female in any male's lineup.

☆

BAD IDEA. YOU should have listened to your gut, Lockwood. If he had, he would be working horses in the ranch arena, penning cattle. Then there would be dinner with fellow ranchers at the monthly cattlemen's meeting. Instead, he would be sitting across the table from Victoria Parker. Somehow the given formal name was popping into his mind a lot more often since she had walked out of her room last night and then today when she shed her outer clothing, and he caught sight of a well-hidden fact… There was an incredible female body hiding away from her constituents. Women in bikinis were nothing new, but the mayor clad in a snug one-piece black suit with cutouts in some interesting places made the springs heat up a bit in his estimation.

And there was something else beginning to intrude into his thoughts. What he had seen so far of the resort and the springs had turned into being a subject that was getting a toehold in his brain. There were possibilities he hadn't thought of…not just those with typical resort planning, but there were the therapeutic benefits at play also. Still, there were reasons he had been adamant against the whole subject in the beginning and still had to be considered. Things had been so much less complicated before one tenacious female had marched up to him one day on his ranch and said she had a business deal for him. And he had ordered her off the ranch. His problem was simple. He should have stuck to that decree and left well enough alone. But here he was, watching that same woman make her exit, this time with sure steps, from the pool. And he stifled a half groan and turned to work off some of his *energy* for the next few minutes. When he next looked in her direction, she had toweled off and wrapped it around her mid-section. She caught his eye and made a hand signal to him that she was heading back to the cabin. He was to take his time.

It was a good idea. He'd do that.

She appeared to be quite dedicated to making things better for people in Destiny's River, but Cade didn't like being on ground that felt more like shifting sand beneath him. It was unsettling and he was a man who didn't like uncertainty in any form. He had gone through that period in his rodeo days when he'd been younger and tried to outride and outrun his responsibilities to his family. He'd made some choices where women were concerned that had taught him a valuable lesson. A sweet-talking, sexy-bodied woman had set her sights on him…or rather his bank account…and he had fallen into a trap. It had taken some dedication and resolve to grow up and get out of the situation. He had escaped her a bit lighter in that bank account. The lesson had been learned. He shook the memory away.

Tori Parker was a different type of female. She was championing a cause that she felt very committed to. That was evident in the sudden change in her when he had simply asked if she had been adopted. And her response was the proverbial slammed door. She wasn't *chosen*.

There was more to her personal story than he was aware. He wasn't being nosy. But he could sense that it meant something deeper to her. And perhaps painful in the bargain? For some reason that thought did not sit at all well within him. She presented such a 'put-together' front in the office of mayor and as a successful businessperson in the community. People couldn't speak well enough of her. And yet, there was something she held on to that caused a pain inside her—and he sensed it, much to his surprise.

Cade climbed out of the pool and began drying off. His thoughts were still twirling around inside his brain. There was the question of the springs and there was the mystery of what was the back story of Tori Parker's life. And why should either of them become of some importance to him?

That was the question he had a feeling he might not want to examine too closely.

He was still mulling things over as he entered the cabin, and noted all was silent as he listened for a shower in the bathroom. She must have taken advantage of being first in and was dressing in her room. Cade gathered up the clothing he would wear for dinner later and moved to the bathroom door. His hand was on the knob when it turned and jerked out of his grasp.

Both stood in shocked surprise for a few moments. Tori stood in the doorway, one hand still on the doorknob and the other secured on the tip of the towel that she had draped around her body like a sarong…a very short sarong. A piece of blue cotton cloth that covered not a lot of her female body.

"Excuse me…" he began.

"Excuse you…" she shot at him at the same time.

"I didn't hear the shower, so I thought you were done and in your bedroom."

"Obviously, you should have knocked. And I am not in my bedroom. If you are finished ogling, you could move out of my way so I might go to my room."

"Ogling?" he mimicked. Her attitude was irritating. "I'm not some teenager who ogles a female. I'm a man who can appreciate the sight of a beautiful woman's body in such a totally unexpected moment."

She narrowed her gaze on him. At the same time he was kicking himself silently for putting that comment out there.

"Beautiful? You're trying to divert my attention with a compliment?"

"It's not a diversion when it's the truth. Take it or leave it. But it might be best if we're both dressed appropriately for any further discussions. Wouldn't you agree?"

She didn't respond except to walk past him with her chin held high and then a sharp slam of her bedroom door.

"Well, that was not your finest hour, Lockwood. An almost naked beautiful woman standing in front of you and what do you do? Stick your boot in your mouth. You'll be lucky if she doesn't poison your food tonight."

☆

WITH HER BACK leaning against the door she'd just slammed, she was berating herself mentally for her behavior. Then she heard his voice, and she listened to the conversation he was obviously having with himself.

Again, the word *beautiful.* Did he need glasses? Or did she need to take a closer look in the mirror? And he was worried she might retaliate with poison? She had to stifle a giggle. Silly man. Who would have thought that Cade Lockwood would ever be tongue-tied? Yet he seemed to be when she'd surprised him. That was most interesting. He had certainly taken a long snapshot in his mind as his gaze had lingered on areas that normally a mayor would not want on public display. She felt a blush forming as she relived the moment. She shouldn't have said a word but retreated to her room immediately. Why didn't she? And the answer that popped into her mind wasn't the one she expected.

Dinner was going to be quite interesting in more ways than one.

Chapter Eight

"WAS THAT THE sound of thunder?" Tori asked the question as she stepped out to the living room. Cade was standing in front of the fireplace. Black slacks had replaced jeans. A deep burgundy long-sleeved shirt with a shiny large gold belt buckle at the waist denoted his world champion status, and the hand-tooled boots when coupled with the black Stetson on his head was more than enough to capture attention, as he looked like he had just stepped out of an advertisement in a western magazine. If she were in the market for a sexy, drop-dead gorgeous cowboy, then he would have her vote. But she wasn't in the market for anything but his agreement on his land and springs. *Keep your eye on the goal and not anything else.*

"In the far distance. There are more storms forecast for after midnight, but they might just skirt around us if we're lucky."

"Then we should get to dinner now just in case."

Tori had chosen a soft cashmere sweater, just a shade lighter than the slacks. She had gathered the long strands of hair upward at the sides of her head and secured them with two gold clips. They complemented the single gold chain with its gold pendant suspended on it and a pair of delicate gold loops for her ears. She had a black suede jacket over her arm and, as she moved to the door, he stepped to join her. She stopped when he reached out and lifted the jacket from her arm.

"There's a chill settling into the valley. Might be best to put this on now." He held it for her to turn around and slide her arms into. She did so after a slight hesitation. Tori settled her hair over the cloth.

"Thank you."

At the bottom of the steps, he offered her his arm and he smiled at her. "The stones are still wet and slippery in spots. We can't have our mayor trying to do all her duties hampered by crutches. Better to be safe than sorry."

She smiled and allowed her hand to lightly rest around his offered arm. Walking side by side with him, she couldn't help noting that the hint of cologne he wore was nice…very nice. These were not things she needed to have on her mind when she needed a clear head for important business matters.

"Good evening. Welcome." The host smiled the greeting as they stepped into the dining room. It was quite a nice atmosphere, given the growing twilight outside the floor-to-ceiling windows where the sun had already slid behind the distant mountain, and clouds were moving in over the valley. The table they were shown was close to the large stone fireplace and with a view also. The crackling fire and the soft glow of the lanterns on the tables gave the room a warm and intimate feeling. Cade held her chair for her and once seated the host handed their menus to them.

"May I get you something from the bar while you look over the menu?"

"Nothing for me except iced tea please," she said. It

would be best to keep her brain focused on the matters at hand.

"I'll have the same as the lady." With drink orders in hand, the host left them alone.

"So, what looks good to you tonight?" she asked, trying to fill any silence.

"Besides my companion?"

Her gaze flew to his face. There definitely was a grin on his face. Was he joking? Why would he say such a thing? "Excuse me?"

"I'm sorry, but not really," he added. "I just thought things felt a bit awkward for some reason and decided I'd try some levity."

"A joke—good to know."

The grin faded. "It wasn't a joke by any stretch of the imagination. I was trying to get you to relax a bit. But you do look lovely tonight and that is a serious statement of fact."

It was good that the waiter arrived with their drinks and Tori could keep her mind on the print in front of her and not the man seated across the table. They both chose salads, steak and accompanying vegetables. The menus were gone and a few more diners had joined them in the dining room, but conversations were muted, and a soft piano was playing some jazz in the bar area across the room from them.

"So, what do you think of what you've seen here?"

"There's no rush. A nice meal and pleasant conversation are usually much better for the digestive system. Business is after."

"If that's what you prefer," Tori agreed. "What would

you consider pleasant conversation?"

"Let's see," he responded. "You get to know your travel companion on trips like this, in most cases. I think it's always good to know more about the person you're spending time with. Don't you agree?"

What was he up to? "In most cases that might be true. But sometimes people doing business with each other might not need to know so much about one another."

"True, but if I'm willing to consider—and note that I said *consider*—changing my opinion on the springs, it might make me more willing to cooperate if I knew more about you."

"Like what exactly? My life is very simple."

"I know you have a sibling brother, our good sheriff. You are the owner of the Primrose Inn. And you are the secret pie lady for the café. Was your family from this area? I think I vaguely remember that you came to Destiny's River several years ago?"

Tori never shied away from her past. She realized a while ago that her life experiences had given her the impetus and basic guts to take what life had dealt and use it to build her inner strength. All of her siblings had done the same. But for some reason, she felt more reticence when it came to this man. It wasn't that she distrusted him with the information, it was something that was harder to explain. But she wasn't going to change her inner beliefs and truths for anyone. She had made that vow when she had decided to step forward and run for public office.

"Yes, I'm not one of those founding members of the community. I arrived here on a bus about twelve years ago. I hadn't planned on this as a destination but the signs were there and my gut told me there would be no other place with such a beautiful sunset, and something told me I had found the home I sought. I haven't once regretted that decision. And my brother felt the same once I talked him into joining me. My other two siblings, a brother and a sister…well I'm still hoping to change their minds one day."

"Our sunset and your gut instinct…that's interesting. There's no doubt that Destiny's River is a place it is hard to leave when you find it. You mentioned you weren't adopted. So, your family…"

"My siblings and I grew up in the foster system for the most part. I never knew my father. Our mother tried as best she could to raise four children. But she wasn't as strong as she wanted to be. We moved in with our grandmother when I was eight and our mother was hit by a drunk driver when she stepped off a bus on the way home from her night job when I was nine. When our grandmother succumbed to cancer, I was thirteen. She had already been in contact with a lawyer who was a neighbor and, long story short, we all went into the foster system with a family ready to help and keep us together. But it can be hard for anyone with two kids of their own and having four added. The caveat had been that we four would either be adopted together or remain together in foster care.

"I don't think it would work that way in this day and time. But we four stuck it out, and let's just say that no one wanted to take us on after meeting us. We had planned that when I aged out, I would look for a place for us. That's why I was on that bus. I saved the money I earned from two jobs as much as possible and I was able to give each sibling a place to call home until they made their own decisions and found their own wings. Many people have much rougher beginnings than we did. Nothing special about our story. No pity needed. It made us who we are today."

"No pity given," he spoke softly. "It's a strength that not many find to use. It does explain some things about you. And I am guilty of misjudging you in my own mind a bit. I own that and apologize."

His words shocked her. This wasn't a man that she could imagine apologizing for much in his life. And yet, he had just made the admission quietly and with sincerity in his steady gaze on her. In that moment, something changed. She didn't know what, but something had sent a ripple through the universe as her younger brother would say. And he was often correct about momentous events in their lives.

"I'm not aware of any need for apologies. But if you feel that is what you need to do, then thank you."

"I think it explains why you have such a positive outlook and why you always see the good in people. And want to make things better for others."

"That would be the bleeding heart some have accused me of having."

"Ah yes…and I might have been one of those when you first announced your campaign."

"You were," she responded with forthrightness, but not accusingly. "I had heard it before and never let it bother me… after the first couple of times. But I just let it add to my determination to stay the course."

"And 'staying the course' can often be a nicer way to say

someone can be stubborn."

"Because I hear a bit of humor in your tone, I won't take that too personally. My brothers are among the few people who can get away with calling me that outright."

"You've had to be someone who takes care of others to a greater degree than most. Makes you overly independent at times so that it becomes a habit."

She stopped before taking the next bite of her dinner. "Why do you suddenly sound like a therapist of some sort?"

"And not a simple cowhand…as you once called me?"

She felt contrition at her own behavior toward him in the past. "You sparked my Irish temper…my grandmother's gift to me. We hadn't gotten off to a good start at our first meeting. I apologize for that reference."

"Accepted." He smiled in return. "Maybe some of that high-priced advice I received the few times I went to a professional sunk into my hard head after all."

"You admit you have a hard head? I am impressed. That seems to be difficult for some males to admit."

"I'm going to regret telling you that, aren't I?" He gave her a rueful smile in return.

"Don't worry. Your secret is safe between you and me," she said. And marveled at how easy a smile came in return. Were they actually talking like two old friends? *Imagine that.*

"I suppose I'll have to trust you on that."

"Once I give my word, I keep it."

"That's good to know." He took a long sip from his glass.

"Do I sense a hint of skepticism?"

He shook his head. "Not really. I've just come across a

few in my time that weren't so forthcoming."

"A few?" She sensed she needed to have her own questions answered. "A few as in women?"

Tori sensed a slight change. Gone was the grin of earlier. Had she misread something?

"Not everyone is as forthright as you. I've come across one or two of those when I didn't know better. A single man is catnip, it seems, around these parts. At least one with a fair-sized bank account."

"I think Matt might agree on part of that."

"Part?"

"A single man…not in the same ballpark in terms of his pocketbook of course…but he is still a good catch and wishes he could just take care of his daughter and his job and leave the rest to chance as he calls it."

"Chance? Like love at first sight?"

"Your tone tells me a lot more than your words. You are one of those men who don't believe in anything so prosaic, evidently."

"And you do…a romantic at heart? I wouldn't have thought you would be one of those women. Waiting for that knight on a horse to come by?"

"I'm afraid I didn't have time for those fairy tales growing up. I just hoped someday a good guy might show up—steady job, family values, patience to put up with me and my work…of course, if he did have a horse in tow, that might seal the deal." She tried to finish on a note meant to bring a smile back to his face. She had to settle for half of one.

"There is that. You do seem to have a thing for animals…small and large ones. Your brother told me about the neon sign above your head, as he calls it. The one that tells all homeless critters that you might be a soft touch?"

"I admit it. I find the company of animals preferable to some humans."

"Guess I might be one of those who fall into that category—you find the company of my horse preferable to me."

She gave it some consideration. "Hmmm...you know, you could be right. Having not met your horse formally though, I will give you the benefit of the doubt."

"I know I should feel honored. And I do."

The waiter appeared with dessert menus. Tori had to shake her head. "I'm afraid I'm too full."

"Well, I should say the same thing, but that double chocolate cake is calling to me. If I can't have one of those pies of yours, then it will have to do for now."

The lightness seemed to have returned between them, and she relaxed with a cup of coffee while her companion enjoyed his dessert. "So, turnabout is fair play. Tell me about the Cade Lockwood I don't know."

"I should have expected this," he said, with a shake of his head. "But fair is fair. It's a simple story. I was born and raised on the Lockwood Ranch, as was my father and his father and his father before him. I think you know that my half sister and I were basically raised by our grandfather. He's why I came back after rodeo was stomped out of my head, and I agreed to take over the ranch's running. My half-sister wanted little part of it, but it did manage to get her set up to follow her own dream, so that turned out okay. I promised my grandfather that I would take care of his legacy and his dreams, and I meant it. Will do so until my last breath. That is the sum total of me."

She shook her head, replacing her coffee cup on the table. "I'm willing to bet there is more, but I do thank you for sharing. And I can hear in your voice and words, your grandfather meant a lot to you."

"And you are correct," he said with a nod. "He's gone, but I still intend to honor his wishes where the ranch is concerned. Do what I believe he would do."

"Well, from what I have seen and heard around the community, you've done that in spades. Which brings an interesting question." She took the gamble. "What would have been his response to my request for use of the hot springs?"

Cade was quiet for a few long moments. His gaze settled on the crackling fire in the fireplace a few feet away, arms folded on the tabletop. He finally turned to fix his gaze upon her.

"I tend to think he would have tanned my hide if he were around to see how bad my manners were the day you arrived at our gate. And I owe you an apology for that behavior. But as far as the springs? I think what he would say needs to stay with me for the time being." The roll of thunder edging closer to their location brought the period to that conversation. He stood.

"We better get a move on, by the sounds of it. Don't want you to have to walk in the rain."

☆

THE WALK BACK to the cabin was more relaxed than the one

they'd taken to dinner earlier. She hadn't hesitated when he'd offered his arm on the return trip. Tori had to smile to herself. It felt almost normal…or it would have in other circumstances. Once inside the cabin, the agenda was back front and center—at least on her mind.

"We still need to discuss the reason we came here. What did you think about the way they've incorporated the springs here?"

He slowly shook his head, as he replaced the fire poker after stoking the fire. "You are most determined. But I'm reserving my opinion until we get back to Destiny's River. And I'd like you to come back to the ranch and for us to take a trip to the springs. I listened to you and your ideas. But now I think you need to listen to me on some things. The best way to do that is to be present on the land. Wouldn't you agree that all sides must be considered?"

Tori hadn't counted on this turn of events. She was disappointed but she shouldn't have been surprised.

"Very well. I see your point."

He gave a slow smile. "I think negotiations are always good. Who knows? You might change your mind."

"And who knows? You might see it in a more positive light after this visit."

He had advanced to stand just in front of her. And she stood her ground. Not sure why she felt she had to do so but backing down had never been her strong suit. She met his gaze, which took a bit of looking upward.

"Or *you* could see things in a different light," he countered. "I can be persuasive too."

Why did she have a sudden desire to ask how persuasive?

That would be crazy. He wasn't a man to push her luck with. That thought was very clear in her brain. But her brain didn't seem to be listening too well. His gaze moved slowly to rest upon her mouth. Did her breathing forget to kick in?

"Negotiating might be very informative in more ways than one." The words were low. Was the fire warming the room too quickly? One of the logs broke, sparks flying about behind the screen. A reminder that a person could get burned if that screen wasn't in place. And her brain kicked in.

"Hold that thought." She stepped away and went to her room. She found what she needed and returned to find him in the same spot. There was an air of expectancy in his stance.

"I have something for you. To help you relax and get a good night's sleep."

An eyebrow raised and the glitter in those blue depths threatened to override her intentions again.

"Here."

He looked down at where she had placed something against his chest.

"What is this?"

"Something you need to give your attention to before we meet again at your ranch. It's some results of my earlier research into this place and two others also, in comparison. To make the best-informed decision, you need facts. So, you can settle in and begin reading. I'll see you bright and early in the morning for the trip home. I have meetings in the afternoon that I cannot miss so we need to get moving as soon as the sun comes up. Have a good evening."

As her door closed behind her, she allowed the breath she had been holding inside to slowly escape. Escape…had she done just that? Well, he might think she ran away. Either way, she remembered just in time why they had come to begin with and what was most important. Let him think what he wanted. She might want him to release the springs to the town but she wasn't going to use any means necessary to obtain his compliance. And if he thought she would, then he would have a long night ahead…with figures of a totally different kind.

Chapter Nine

"DID YOU FIND all your facts?"

Matt's question caught her off guard. Which had happened more than once in the two days since her return from the trip with Cade. "What do you mean?"

"You said you were going on a fact-finding mission. So, what fact did you find out? Did you and Cade discover any common ground?"

Common ground? Shaky ground would be a better description. And nothing to do with the springs issue. But she wasn't going to say that to her brother. "We're still discussing the issue."

Matt grinned but kept his attention on the plate of nachos in front of him. He wasn't fooling Tori though. He was her brother after all, and she knew from past experiences that he could feign ignorance of something with the best of them.

"I see."

Tori gave her brother one of those big sister looks that had always served her well in the past. Except it didn't this time. "What are you inferring?"

"Me? Who said I was *inferring* anything? We lawmen don't do a lot of *inferring*. We look at evidence and make flat-out statements."

"Then make a statement if you think you're so smart."

He settled his gaze upon her. "Well, now that you've asked. It's fairly simple deducing."

She shook her head. "I have a feeling you're about to find your deducing skills are not all that sharp all the time."

"I believe that both of you did find some common ground on the springs issue. Because *you* wouldn't have it any other way. However, I believe that you both agreed to keep discussing the matter because there are other things that came up during this trip. Let's say you two didn't come back as the combatants you left. Which is why I saw the man twice…once yesterday and once today and both times he asked how my sister was doing. He has never done that before as we both well know."

"You are way off base, Matthew."

"And you never call me Matthew unless I've really gotten under your skin."

"I would change the subject if I were you," she added, giving him the look.

"One last bit of evidence," he said. "The man just walked in the door and was going to another direction until he spied you. Smile, sis…he's heading straight for you." Matthew said the last words while putting a welcoming smile on his face and outstretching his hand.

Why did her stomach squeeze and a sense of panic set in? *Get a grip.* She would have two pairs of prying eyes on her now. She hoped the smile on her face was not as shaky as she was feeling as she met those blue eyes, and he shook hands with Matt.

"Good to see you, Cade. Care to join us?"

Tori wished she could give a swift kick to her brother's

leg beneath the table at that moment. He'd issued the invite on purpose. There was nothing for it but to lift a smile at the cowboy who stood beside their table.

"Good afternoon, Matt. And to you, Mayor." His voice and demeanor gave nothing away but a casual greeting. That seemed to irritate her more than it should have. But if they were back to their usual selves in Destiny's River, then so be it. She nodded and said a brief: "Afternoon Mr. Lockwood."

He had already turned his attention back to Matt. "Thanks for the invite but I'm meeting someone, and I see she's already been seated toward the back and is waiting on me. Maybe another time. Have a good lunch." He left them and Matt reclaimed his seat.

Tori itched to turn around and see who the 'she' was he had mentioned. But that would be too noticeable, especially by her brother. However, it didn't keep him from giving an account of what he saw.

"My, my…so he does have a very nice-looking lunch partner if my eyesight doesn't deceive me. I wonder who she is? I would remember her if she was from these parts."

Tori kept her focus on the salad in front of her. "If you're so interested, then go introduce yourself. She might find the badge lends you some sort of country charm."

"Meow," he commented, looking across at his sister. "That sounded almost catty on your part, but then why should it? Evidently you don't have any particular interest in the man…even after you two took a trip together."

Tori shook her head. "It takes a good deal of patience to be your sister. And I'm not the one ogling them."

"I am not ogling. I am, after all, a single man who appreciates a beautiful woman when he sees one. And looks like Cade does, also. They are having a very deep conversation…heads close together, gazes locked on each other. Yep, she might be a keeper."

"I have had my fill," she said, placing her napkin beside her plate. "I believe you said lunch was on you, so I'll leave you to it. Give Jilliebean my love. We'll go shopping next weekend as promised." Tori made a concerted effort not to glance in a certain direction as she moved toward the doorway. And she almost made it, but Leslie Wright—a member of the council—stopped her as she was almost to the doorway.

"There you are, Tori," she said. "I was going to call you later, but I know you're a busy woman. Then I saw you here and might as well strike while I can. We wanted to get your opinion on something we want to try for the October Fest list of events. We think it will make quite a good deal of funds for the furniture for the addition to the children's play area in the hospital."

"Sounds interesting. What is it?"

"A bachelor auction! Isn't that fun? Only we might call it something like Cowboy Roundup or something fitting in with the western theme, or we could even do something like masks and masquerade…but what do you think of the idea?"

Tori had not planned on having this conversation with the woman in the café. She wanted to distance herself from the vicinity of Cade and his lunch date.

"Let's step outside and free up space for this lunch crowd. Or you can call me later and tell Wallace I asked you to call." She began moving to the door. Once outside, she felt she was home free but that thought had come too soon.

"Tori, just one more thing," Leslie said, having hustled outside right after her. "Another option to think about is why not make it an auction for both men and women? Wouldn't want to leave anyone out. Of course, it would be notable members of the community who we would ask to volunteer to be auctioned. It could be such fun!"

"That's quite an idea," Tori responded, moving slowly yet determinedly farther away from the café. "Why don't you run it by the event committee members, get their input, have a vote and then if all are of the same mind, you can bring it before the council next Monday evening with all the specifics attached."

"That would be wonderful. I am so glad that we can count on your support. And you know, we must add both you and your brother's names to our list of auction stars. And we will line up others before the meeting, also. I am just so excited now…thanks, Mayor!" She hurried off and Tori felt relief. She crossed the street in the direction of the courthouse. As she was about to enter the building, she caught sight of the familiar black truck—for once, not parked in her reserved spot. And Cade and his companion had just arrived between it and a convertible parked next to it.

Tori stepped inside slowly but not so much so that she couldn't see the couple. They stood for a few moments talking, then the woman stretched on tiptoe and gave the tall cowboy a hug. Which he returned easily, even adding a brief kiss on the cheek before opening the female's door for her and shutting it once she was comfortably inside. And that is all Tori needed to see.

None of my business. He was a grown man. They both appeared old enough to be consenting adults. Why did it matter in the least? Tori had appointments to keep and she headed upstairs to her office. But her mind wouldn't vacate the scene she had witnessed outside a few minutes earlier. The woman obviously wasn't a stranger to Cade Lockwood. But she wasn't someone local…Tori had not met her before. She would certainly remember if she had. And Matt was in the dark about her identity also. Her car was an expensive luxury model as were the fuchsia cowl-necked sweater and black slacks with her long black hair as shiny as a raven's wing. She reeked of money. Tori shouldn't be surprised. That would be the type of woman who would attract a wealthy rancher like Cade Lockwood. Money attracts money.

"Lunch not sit well?"

Tori had sat her shoulder bag down with a thud on the edge of her desk. She took a seat on her chair behind her desk, swinging around to face the window behind her. Wallace's question brought clarity back to her thoughts. She turned the chair around to face her assistant.

"Sorry, just a lot on my mind about what I need to accomplish today. Let's get the reports for the proposed street work on the east side. We need to be up to speed when the engineers bring in their budget proposal."

"Will do." He turned to leave and then stopped. "By the way, Mr. Lockwood has called twice now and would like to schedule some time with you today. I did tell him you were busy, but I thought I would run it by you just in case you wanted to try to fit him in?"

"No," she said in response. "My schedule is full. And it will be tomorrow also...and the next. He just can't call at the last minute and expects to be fitted into our workday. He is not to be treated any different than anyone else in this town."

"I see. Well then, I shall handle that." He closed the door behind him.

Great way to handle that. But he just couldn't expect any favors from her office. Let other women rearrange their schedules for him. *What is your problem?*

And as soon as she asked that of herself, she slammed the door before an answer could wreck the rest of her day.

✯

"I TOLD YOU to wait until I could get over there and take care of those leaves."

Tori stood on the second-to-top rung of the ladder, balancing her cell phone between her shoulder and ear, while she tried to reach the clump of leaves and debris that was lodged just at the top of the drainage pipe from the gutter on the corner of her covered porch. She had managed to remove the first clump, but the next one was giving her some issues. She was already as high as she wanted to go on the ladder. It had seemed an easy project to handle when her brother had to cancel at the last minute for an issue in his office. Surely, she had told herself, she could handle such a project and be done with it.

"I am not helpless, and I have almost got this. But I need

to get off the phone with you to do it. Now go be sheriff and let me finish this. Bye."

She clicked off and the phone slipped. She tried to make a saving grab for it but the ladder shifted a bit and it was either save the phone or jump for it. The phone made a thud when it hit the grass. Thankfully it looked in one piece. But her nerves weren't. Her fingers gripped the edges of the ladder until she was certain it wasn't going to move again. Maybe just one more step upwards and she could get the whole thing over with.

"Are you crazy? Get down from there before you drop something besides your phone."

The voice shocked her, and her foot missed the rung. Just when she thought she was done for, a solid frame of warm body was right behind her on the ladder, breaking any chance of her fall. Then she looked over her shoulder, and her worst expectations were confirmed.

"What are you doing on my ladder? You scared me and I could have fallen."

"Excuse me, but you did not fall because I managed to get up here and keep that from happening. Any falling from a ladder would be *your* fault for being up here in the first place."

Being pressed between the hard metal of the ladder and the hard male body behind her was the last place she needed to be. *Try to maintain some semblance of composure.*

"This is neither a place for a lecture nor a discussion. Kindly get down so that I might get off this thing."

He slowly backed down and waited for her descent. *Fine mess. Certainly not the finest moment of her life. So much for a graceful exit.*

She made it down and tried to gather her usual business composure. It was a little hard to do when that blue gaze was definitely not going anywhere.

"What is it that you want? I don't usually conduct business in my backyard after hours."

"Well, I haven't had a lot of luck getting an audience with your highness doing it the usual business way. So I was in the neighborhood and luckily caught sight of you dangling from this ladder. You might say I'm taking care of two problems at the same time and should be getting a thank you at least."

"Thank you? I didn't ask you to stop and help. Let's get that clear. I was doing okay until you snuck into my yard and scared me."

"So, we're back to square one, are we?"

"Square one?"

"You being your uptight, high and mighty mayor self and me being a tax-paying citizen, being treated not very amiably by you. I did try to make appointments with you like you requested, but for some reason your schedule seems to be a bit stuffed lately. And you seem to have forgotten how to return phone calls. I thought you were trying to get me on board with your springs idea. This is not boding well for that."

"Look..." She tried to take a deep breath and get control of a situation that was clearly about to escalate, but his mention of the springs brought perspective. *Don't blow it.*

"I have been busy since we returned. And I should have spent more time trying to return all the calls that had piled up during the last couple of days. But I was going to finish getting to them tomorrow. And while I wish there were more hours in the day, I do have a home I have to try and take care of, which also coincides with my business of being an innkeeper also. The gutters are causing issues after the last rain and I needed to handle it. Sorry you had to take time from your busy schedule to bring your issue to my doorstep…after hours."

He had listened. And maybe his broad shoulders didn't seem quite as rigid as they first appeared, and there was a bit of relaxing in that strong jawline. And she shouldn't be watching him so closely.

"I see. Well, all of us are entitled to have an off day now and then, I suppose. And I should have alerted you to my presence in your yard before just jumping on your ladder. But I thought you were about to take a tumble, and I tried to prevent that. Sorry for scaring you."

He was apologizing? Mark the calendar.

Then she felt contrite for being so catty in her thoughts. "Thank you. I'm sorry for overreacting. I appreciate you for keeping my bones in one piece."

There was a hint of a smile at the corner of his mouth and that was also not something she should be looking at. After all, there was someone else who had a claim to that area. She better not forget that fact.

His hand lifted and two fingers brushed the side of her head, bringing everything into sharp focus. Before she could back away or react, his fingers drew back with two leaves that had been stuck in her hair. And she felt even worse as the last vestiges she tried to project of being halfway better-looking than she felt, were literally plucked away.

"Thanks," she said, as it came out in just better than a mumble. "What was it that you needed to speak to me about?"

"I'll tell you if you promise that you will not get back on that ladder after I'm gone."

"Just tell me."

"I was going to ask if you would come out to the ranch this Saturday and we can go up to the springs and finish our discussion with my point of view added into it. We saw the springs on our trip, and you certainly gave me a lot of research to read through, which I have. Now you need to see my perspective...correct?"

She couldn't deny that fact. "Yes, that is true. And I'll be able to come out in the afternoon if that's agreeable?"

"Yes, that's fine. My people will be expecting you and they'll let me know when you arrive. Let's say two o'clock?"

She nodded.

"Good. And now I'll just put this ladder back in the garage for you and be on my way. It's getting too dark out here to be working anyway." And he did just that. The nerve of him. She hadn't asked him to help.

"Look, I can do that."

He didn't stop. With the ladder over his shoulder, he strode to the open garage, and all was done in a couple of minutes.

"All done. Now I have an engagement to get to, so I'll leave you. See you Saturday, Mayor."

She tried not to but watching him walk down the driveway to his truck was something she couldn't resist doing. He turned and caught her and he grinned, touching a finger to the brim of his hat. The truck roared to life, and he was gone.

"He probably thinks I was ogling those tight jeans. Him and his Texas-sized ego." She was speaking to only herself. Add that to making her feel even more ridiculous in her jeans with patches and an old work shirt of her brother's. Leaves in her hair. Probably dirt smears too. Not exactly her finest moment. And in comparison, to how his *engagement* was probably going to look this evening, she would be the comic relief for him.

Well, she was who she was. No use trying to be any other way. Cade Lockwood was not in her realm. And that thought made her feel worse instead of better. *Darn him!*

Chapter Ten

"WELL, LOOK HERE...TWO of my favorite customers. Must be looking for some of those blueberry pancakes I think about ready to come off the griddle. Am I right?" Tillie Newberry, owner of Tillie's Café and Bakery, welcomed her latest customers as they took their preferred places in one of the front booths. It was a sunny Saturday morning and the bell above the front door was almost constantly ringing as more customers entered. Tillie's was the place to begin your day as far as most people in Destiny's River would attest.

"Right as always." Tori smiled in greeting.

"And a glass of chocolate milk, too, if you please."

"Miss Jillie Parker, you have grown another foot since I last saw you a week ago, I do believe." The woman grinned at the child...all of six years old but often seeming to be going on sixteen in her behavior and level of youthful wisdom.

"I wish," the child replied. "I want to be able to play basketball with my dad's team but I'm too short."

Tillie laughed. "You'll get there, sweetie. Don't be in such a hurry to grow up. Enjoy these days."

"That's what my dad says and my aunt Tori."

"And they are both very smart people. Look at your aunt

here…the mayor of this town no less. And what will the mayor be having? Your usual? Two slices of crisp bacon, one egg scrambled hard and two of Delbert's homemade sourdough biscuits…with country gravy, of course?"

"It's Saturday and I'm spending part of it with my favorite niece here shopping so yes, I need a big breakfast for energy to keep up with her."

"And a mug of coffee, too," Tillie added. "I'll get these orders in and be back with your drinks."

"Are you excited about your concert tomorrow?"

The child nodded. "I guess so. Do you think we can find a pretty dress today? Maybe something for my hair, too?"

"I believe we'll find all of that and more. You are making your solo debut and that requires an extra-special outfit as well."

"I'm nervous. What if I forget my part?"

"You won't forget. And being nervous is all part of a good performance. Once you get up there, with all your friends, and Mrs. Caspell, your director, it will feel perfect, and you just open your mouth and sing. Just like in all your rehearsals. The audience is made up of all the people you know and have known you for all your life. They are there to support you, too."

The smile returned to the child's face at the same time Tillie returned with their drink order.

"Are you going to come to the choir concert tomorrow afternoon?"

"I certainly am, Miss Jillie. I wouldn't miss it. Because I hear a special young lady will be doing a solo and I certainly want to hear it."

Tori sat back and sipped her coffee, watching the exchange between the two. She loved her niece something fierce. Matt's child had grown up surrounded by so many good people there in Destiny. Jillie had been born after a difficult birth. A birth that had claimed her young mother's life and left her brother a single dad with a newborn. Luckily, they had been blessed by a community that drew them into their hearts and surrounded them with help in whatever they needed. She had been the first one to christen the little girl with her nickname of *Jilliebean*...an offshoot of jellybean. As a baby, she had been so tiny, and Tori had joked she was no more than the size of a jellybean. She then became her little Jilliebean...a child she had given her heart to in an instant. Matt had evolved from the beginning into a great dad. She had done her best to step in to a surrogate mother role whenever needed. And today, they would be shopping for the perfect outfit for her first solo in a choir concert in the afternoon after church.

"Well, here we are, special delivery for Miss Jillie Parker, Destiny's up-and-coming singing sensation." The white-jacketed cook delivered their food to the table himself and with a flourish of hands, set the plates in front of them. "Eight silver-dollar-sized fluffy pancakes with extra blueberries in each because we treat our special customers right here at Tillie's." He gave a wink and headed back to his kitchen.

"Yes, we do," Tillie agreed. "You ladies enjoy and I'll see you tomorrow."

Twenty minutes later, with an excited Jillie leading the way, they exited onto the main street and began their shopping expedition. The third shop they entered, The

Purple Lion, was the jackpot winner.

Three outfits into the search, the winner turned out to be a deep purple velvet jumper over a white silk blouse with puffy sleeves caught in at the wrist with cuffs and a large white bow at the collar. They added white tights. And the best part was a purple velvet hair bow and a pair of purple slip-ons in a shiny material. Jillie turned this way and that in front of the full-length mirror. Her big brown eyes sparkled with anticipation.

"It's so soft and pretty," she breathed. "Daddy will like it, too, don't you think?"

"I think it's perfect and your daddy may shed a tear or two when he sees how grown up his little girl looks all dressed up in such a pretty outfit."

The smile dimmed a bit on the child's face as she continued to look at her reflection in the mirror. She had grown quiet.

Tori stood and moved to stand behind her, hands on her shoulders as she caught her gaze in the mirror in front of them. "Where did that pretty smile go, Jilliebean?" she asked softly. "What's up? And don't say nothing."

"It's just…I just…do you think my dad will ever get married again?"

"Wow," Tori said, meeting the somber gaze in the mirror. "So did something happen to put this question in your brain?"

"Not really. I just heard Missy and Roxie were going shopping today with their moms and having a sleepover and all. And I guess I just wanted to know what that's like…having a mom to do that with." Then she grew wide-eyed and swung around to face Tori.

"I'm sorry. It's not because you aren't fun, and this isn't fun because you do all kinds of stuff with me and all but…"

"But I'm not your own mom," Tori finished for her. "I get it. And it doesn't hurt my feelings. I remember how much I would dream about what it would be like to have my mom there to do things with like other kids did. Don't ever apologize for wanting that for yourself. And who knows…if the right person comes along, maybe your dad might want to marry again. But no matter what, we will both be here for you always."

"I love you, Aunt Tori. You're the best." The hug was a good one.

"Love you more, little one. Now let's get all your goodies and get to my house so your dad can pick you up. I have some work I have to do this afternoon."

☆

"WHAT IS ALL of this?" Tori asked, as she exited her SUV a few minutes later. Matt was standing at the edge of the sidewalk with an amused look on his face.

"You had no idea?"

"Idea about what? Who are these men? What have you done?"

His hands shot up. "Don't look at me. I had nothing to do with this. I found them about to load up when I arrived just a few minutes ago. I'll let you ask that question of the foreman." He waved to one of the men who had just finished loading up some materials in the back of his truck. The man came over, removing his hat and extending his hand to Tori.

"Afternoon ma'am. I'm Nate Hastings. I work at Lockwood Ranch. Me and some of our work crew was sent over to help with your gutters and we did a little repair on the back steps that needed it. They're very safe now."

"Lockwood? You're from the Lockwood Ranch?" It was beginning to dawn on her.

"You'll have to forgive my sister, Nate." Matt was grinning. "She is a little slow on the uptake sometimes."

Tori shot him a look while she shook hands with the ranch hand. "I had no idea this was happening," she explained to the man. "But thank you and all of your men for the work. It is much appreciated."

"You are welcome, ma'am, and we'll be on our way now."

"What is the bill for all of this? How do I…"

He shook his head. "No ma'am, no bill. It's with Mr. Cade's compliments is what he said to tell you when you tried to pay us. He had an idea you would ask."

"I see. Well, I'll discuss it with him then."

"Have a good day." The trucks with the crew were soon on their way down the driveway.

Matt and Jillie stood watching her.

She smiled at Jillie. "Sweetie, why don't you run and put your packages in your dad's truck? He will be with you in just a few minutes."

After another tight hug, the girl headed off with both hands full of her shopping items.

"Looks like you two had fun with my credit card today," Matt observed.

Tori turned to face him. "We did not touch your card. This was a gift from her favorite aunt today."

"Her favorite? You're her only aunt."

"Don't even try to change the subject. And don't even try to make any smart remarks about what happened here today."

"What?" His act of innocence would not have won an Oscar. "Just because I arrive to find a Lockwood work crew scurrying around here like some fairy godmother team? Wanting to be done before you arrived. I would say that you and Cade did indeed bury the hatchet on that little trip you two took."

"Burying a hatchet sounds good right about now," she commented with one of her sister warning looks. "Quit while you still can."

"Well, I'll just be on my way, since I'm sure you want to get ready for your meeting at the Lockwood Ranch this afternoon. You might try something a little less mayor-looking and more…"

"Do not finish that sentence," she broke in.

"Thanks again for taking Jillie shopping. I can't wait to hear how this meeting goes." He was moving toward his truck and added the last just as he closed his door…safe and soundproof inside the vehicle.

☆

TORI HADN'T PLANNED on changing outfits but then she did decide to bake two pies to take to the crew at the ranch, by way of saying thanks again for their work. So she did need to change because there was a speck of flour on one pantleg.

Two hours later, she was pulling up to the iron gate with the arch above with the Lockwood brand in its center. This time, the gate opened without her saying a word into the speaker box. Evidently, the camera was in use. It was a far different entrance than the last one where she had to beg practically until the poor cowboy on the opposite side of the gate finally allowed her to pass through.

There was time for one more look in the mirror to check the soft shade of rose lipstick that she had added at the last minute. After going through four outfits she finally gave up and decided that she felt silly. She was heading to a ranch where she would no doubt be going through bushes and whatever else to make her way to the springs, so a nice outfit was out. She settled on a pair of dark blue jeans, a pullover sweater in light blue and a sleeveless vest in denim. A dark red scarf was wound casually around her neck. She was tempted to leave her hair down, but at the last minute she smoothed it into the usual ponytail. With a recurring image of the woman and the kiss she'd witnessed Caden give her a few days ago, she reminded herself that it was just a business meeting and nothing else. And that was okay with her.

The house came into view. It was a beautiful, natural stone, one-story home. Its long length lent itself to a porch that ran the length of the front. Comfy patio furniture with fall colors made it seem inviting along with urns of yellow, gold and orange mums. It wasn't the mansion that most people might have expected but it did declare wealth in a classic, understated way.

A housekeeper opened the door to her knock. She was

about to step inside, as the housekeeper took the two pie carriers from her hands, when they heard the approach of horses. It was her host. And she schooled herself to not get lost in the fact that Cade Lockwood on horseback was pretty hard to tear your gaze away from. She failed though. Especially when he swung out of the saddle and strode toward her, that smile appearing that she was certain had been the downfall of many a woman over his years in rodeo.

"Punctual as always," he said to her as he joined her on the porch. He glanced at his housekeeper. "Could those be pies in Mrs. Jones's hands? You baked them for me?"

"Yes, they are pies I just baked. But they're for the workmen who somehow appeared at my house today. They did a very good job…even though they shouldn't have come at all. So the least I could do was bake them something."

He only smiled and nodded at Mrs. Jones. "Please see that those go to Nate and his crew, with the heartfelt gratitude of our mayor."

She left them and Tori wished she had stayed around longer. Which was ridiculous because she had handled many business meetings with men just as important as Cade Lockwood and did just fine holding her own. But this was different. How different, she was about to find out.

"Well, we don't want to waste daylight. And we're supposed to have some rain later coming in from the southwest. So, let's get on our way to the springs. I chose a gentle mount for you."

He was headed back down the steps. She stayed in her spot. "Mount?"

Cade took the reins of a beautiful gray mare in his hands.

She had been patiently waiting next to his big black horse. "The springs aren't in walking distance. And since I found out how much you love horses, I thought this might be a treat for you. I promise Ladybug is a perfect lady." He held out the reins to her.

Tori knew she was being had…again, by the cowboy. He knew that it would be hard for her to look into those beautiful large doe eyes of the animal and not melt. That and the fact she had always wanted her own horse…he was not playing fair. She still didn't take the reins.

"Take your left hand and rub down her nose from her forehead—she really likes that. Don't be afraid."

"I'm not afraid," she corrected him. She eased forward and lifted her hand. The mare stood still, patiently waiting. She slid her hand down slowly along the ridge of the horse's nose. She looked into those eyes and instantly fell in love.

"Ladybug," she said softly, making another long stroke down to the velvet-soft skin around her nostrils. "You are such a beautiful lady with a perfect name. You are a real sweetheart for certain."

"Take the reins in your right hand and we'll get you in the saddle." Cade's voice was low as he stood next to her.

"You put your left foot in the stirrup—she isn't going to move. And I've got her also. Then take a little jump to lift yourself upward, your right leg swinging over her back. On three."

She counted in her mind as he counted aloud and in one movement, she realized she wasn't standing on the ground any longer but seated on the back of a horse. And it was amazing…just like she had imagined in all her childhood dreams. Only this was reality.

"Take the reins and don't worry, she won't move until you tell her." He moved with a swift confidence, much smoother than her first attempt, he was in the saddle of his mount. He drew in beside her.

"I won't soon forget the look on your face right now."

"Abject fear?"

"Undeniable joy is what comes to mind. You look good in the saddle. Let's see how you do when we start walking them. Watch my light tapping of the sides of my horse and you do the same."

"You said walk, right? We don't need to go faster." She followed Cade's direction and Ladybug began a slow walk. And that's how it went for the next half hour. Cade would give instructions and then she would follow. It was such an amazing feeling that before she knew it, they had progressed from a slow cadence to a rocking one and then to a faster trot. And each step she found herself wanting to go even faster. But Cade was a good teacher and kept his pupil on target.

They topped a rise and came down to the banks of a running stream. They halted. Cade swung out of the saddle and moved to take Ladybug's reins from her. He instructed her on how to dismount and she did so. But he left out the part where her legs might feel a bit like rubber. Luckily, he was there to catch her arm and right her until she was steady on her feet.

"You survived. Good job. We'll let them enjoy some water and rest while we take a little walk and let you get your land legs back."

"Aren't we going to tie them up?" The horses were already enjoying the water.

"They are trained to stay where their reins are dropped. A good ranch horse learns that before much else. Let's take a walk."

She was still basking in the joy over having ridden a horse...and survived. So she didn't pull away when he offered a hand to provide a steadying support on her elbow.

The trees were much taller as they progressed along the edge of the stream. Then they took a turn and went up a little rise.

"Oh my," Tori breathed out the words as she took in the beauty of the spot before her. A large, clear pool was just below them. She could see all the way to the bottom the water was so pure and clear. Then as it deepened, it became an amazing shade of blue. Looking farther, she could see another pool just like it, and that was emptying a steady stream of water down into the first pool.

"These are the springs?"

"These are the first set of springs," he corrected. "I take it that you're impressed."

"The beauty and the tranquility is amazing. It's even more perfect than I imagined. The photos I saw do not do it justice."

"This is where Destiny's River begins. Where my great-great-grandfather settled his family. And where each generation of Lockwood has begun their protection of them."

"I can see why you feel so protective of them. There is something special about this place. You can feel it."

He was looking at her in such a way that she felt her

breath slow to almost nothing. His gaze was drawing her into some unknown world within it. "I knew you were going to be trouble, Victoria Parker. Now I understand what my grandfather meant about the first woman he brought to these springs."

She made no move when he slowly raised his hand to cup the side of her head. His palm held a warmth that felt like the warmth of coming home on a chilled evening. That thought flashed through her brain just as his head dipped to hers and his lips touched hers. Warm, tempting hers to join in a pleasure like no other. Then they were gone. His hand returned to his side. The silence was deafening.

"My grandfather was right." The words were low, and did she imagine he had even spoken them? Did he mean to speak them aloud? What was happening?

Chapter Eleven

HAVE YOU LOST your mind?

Caleb was transported to another moment, standing at the springs alongside his grandfather. A teenage version of himself and a wise, older man. He had joked that the spot would be great to add a slide to it and have more people able to enjoy some fun in the spot.

"That's not for this spot, and you need to understand that." The tone of his grandfather's voice was one he'd rarely heard in all the years he'd been old enough to understand things. Then he should have let it drop, but he didn't.

"What is so special about this spot, Grandfather? You have said that over the years, but I don't understand why. You've always said I wasn't old enough to understand. I'm nineteen now. I'm older than others my age—you've said that yourself. I need to understand."

Grandfather stood silently, his gaze on the springs and beyond. Cade was about to give up ever getting an answer of any consequence from the man. Then he began to speak, focusing on some point unseen to Cade.

"I married your grandmother, but she was not the one who owned my heart. And you know that throughout the years, I gave my best to your grandmother. She wanted for nothing, and we had a good marriage—not one born of a grand passion or the fragile foundation of hearts, but still solid on respect and caring."

Cade had never expected to hear those words. He was transfixed into silence.

"There was a girl from high school. Her family came to Destiny's River when her father was transferred here to build the new bank in town. She was quiet, but the moment I saw her and she turned and smiled...something reached inside me and flipped a switch. I had only been going through the motions in life until then. She had a way of seeing life with joy and feeling...even though her home life wasn't the best, I would learn, she never let life get the best of her. She made her own clothes so that certainly gave the girls in town something to think less of her about. When we had a school dance, she didn't come. I didn't know why. But then I saw her sitting alone under that old oak tree beside the swimming hole we had in town. We talked and talked, and before I knew it that had settled my path.

"Except it wasn't the accepted one, the one my parents expected of me. I had to make a choice. I had told them that I loved her and wanted to make a life with her. They began telling me that we were too young to know what we wanted or to be in love. But they were wrong. Anyway, we took a picnic lunch up here, to these springs. They had become our special escape from all those voices. She loved them. And it was she who first asked me to preserve this spot, no matter what. And I have, and it will be up to you when I'm gone and you take over this land to hopefully honor that request also."

"What happened?" Cade asked. "Why didn't you marry

her? Did your family talk you out of it?"

"No, I was prepared to walk away from this land, away from my family. But Annie knew better. She said that it would become the biggest regret of my life if I did that. And she would want no part of that. But I was hardheaded and made plans to leave with her." He was silent for a moment. It clearly still brought pain to the man who Cade thought impervious to such things.

"Annie left Destiny's River. She left me a note saying she couldn't take me away from my destiny here on this land. She knew that we could never have a future because of it. So, she was leaving and asked me not to look for her. She would always love me, but she knew I needed to realize that this land was deeper ingrained in me than any other love could be. So, I let her go. My pride was hurt, and I stayed here. I did what was needed for our family and this ranch. But there was never a day when I wouldn't find my way here to this spot. And remember the first time I brought her to the springs. I knew my heart had found its home with her that moment. And she took it with her when she left."

"And you kept your promise to her ever since to keep the springs the way they were when she asked you for that promise."

"I shared this with you so you can understand why I ask that you do what is right."

Cade had never forgotten that day. And he could now also grasp what his grandfather had felt when he had stood beside the same springs and looked into the eyes of a woman who would have such an impact on his life. It was a sobering and eye-opening moment with the past fusing with the present.

☆

"WE CAN TALK back at the house. The sky is getting darker, and the wind is picking up. We need to get a move on." This time he didn't lend a helping hand to her as they headed back down the path to where the horses stood. He held the reins while she mounted Ladybug. Then he did the same and turned his horse toward their return. Tori followed in silence. What had just happened was hard to process. It was unexpected. And yet, she had to own the fact that she hadn't objected. And what had he meant by his words about his grandfather? Had he even realized he had spoken them? And while it wasn't the first kiss she had ever received, it was one that had made feelings come alive inside her in such a way that shocked her.

Tori wasn't one to play with emotions. And she certainly didn't care for anyone playing with hers. Or maybe she was taking it too seriously? Maybe Cade Lockwood was used to females hugging him on a public street every day? Whatever was the case, he needed to know that she wasn't interested in joining the line of candidates.

The raindrops began just as they reached the first barn. They rode inside out of the rain before he stopped them. He went inside one of the rooms and came out with a soft Indian blanket and handed it to her.

"You're liable to feel a chill given you got a bit damp out there and the air has a bite to it. Use this to warm up. It's really pouring right now so we'll sit it out and wait for it to break. In the meantime, I'll rub down the horses and put them up."

Tori felt bad about sitting there while he unsaddled them. She stepped over to Ladybug who was waiting patiently for her turn. Watching Cade's movements, she found another brush and laid it down until she could get the hang of unbuckling the saddle. Once that was done, she was about to take the saddle off but Cade stepped up at that moment. He grabbed under the saddle horn and at the back of the saddle and lifted it with one easy movement, setting it on a nearby sawhorse. She slid the blanket off the horse's back and draped it over the saddle. Ladybug was led to her stall next. Tori watched while her bridle was removed and hung on a peg next to the stall door.

While the horses were chowing down from their feed buckets, they each had a brush and they began the brushing that was clearly okay as far as the animals were concerned. Once that was done, he checked outside and the rain was still not letting up.

Cade tossed a couple of fresh hay bales out of range of the water. He indicated she could sit on them.

"We might as well use this time to discuss the springs."

That was a topic she could engage in and did so. "What is the reason you are against it? Too many people? We can set daily limits. The road needs to be worked on to handle traffic? The city and county are willing to provide their services. You wouldn't be out a dime. As far as facilities such as restrooms? We can use portables until our crews can construct permanent ones. We are prepared to take on quite a bit of expense in order to help make this happen. What is left that you think is a barrier?"

"My grandfather's wishes. He didn't want to see crowds

coming into a spot that clearly meant something very special to him and his life. He safeguarded its pristine beauty and peace all his life. And he made me promise to do the same."

"Evidently, the springs were really special in some way to him. And I can appreciate that. But for those people who would be coming here for the springs as part of their medical needs, well wouldn't that mean something to him also? We can limit those who come here daily. We..."

Cade held up a palm. "I was very much opposed to opening and for much the same reasons my grandfather had. But there are other ways to handle things that weren't in his ability to consider before. And time...well time has passed. Grandfather passed. I did hear his concerns and the reason why he wanted things left the way they have been for decades. But he also trusted me to know if and when the time came for there to be another way to use their benefits."

"You said you *were* opposed? Does that mean you might be changing your mind?"

"Not so much as changing my mind as realizing that times have moved on. And seeing the springs we visited this past week opened my mind to one or two things that might have swayed my grandfather's opinion in one way. It is something I might be able to get behind."

"I'm listening."

"Are you warm enough? I can get you another blanket." His consideration touched something in her. It felt nice. But then she remembered, and it was time to keep her mind and eyes on the prize to be had.

"Thank you, but I'm fine. You were saying?"

"Always the mayor," he commented. "Business before

anything else. Very well."

Let him think what he wanted. She could take exception to his remarks some other time.

"You pointed out in some of that thick folder of paperwork that you left with me to read a few days back, something that stuck with me and seemed to reinforce what had come to mind a couple of times before when this discussion about the springs first began.

"Setting aside the recreational use of the pools, let's talk about the health value. You had a couple of studies and testimonies from the area doctors and hospitals in a hundred-mile radius. I found those numbers and their arguments quite interesting. And I coupled that with the two people, especially the child and his family, that we spoke with while visiting the springs. It stayed with me."

"Yes." She nodded. "The health value of the thermal springs found here among the pools can be of major value in physical therapy and rehabilitation of patients with a variety of needs."

"I believe they were somewhat helpful to my grandfather in his physical ailments."

"Somewhat? Did he have an incurable disease?"

"Incurable disease? Some might think so…he did. But in the true sense of those words…not really. He lost what he believed to be the love of his life. And from then on, he was a different man…with a broken, half-empty heart he said once. I was younger and not fully able to understand what he really meant. But with age, perhaps a bit of wisdom came along."

The story touched Tori's heart. "I'm sorry for him that

he had to experience that. It's very sad."

"You are a romantic…something else I've learned about you."

"We were discussing the springs," she said bringing him back to the subject at hand and away from anything personal. "What is your thinking on allowing use of the springs?"

"I might be considering allowing *limited* use," he began and then held up his hand. "Now don't go getting too excited or ahead of things. I said *considering*."

"I'll take it. It's a positive."

"You don't give up easily on something, do you?"

"I learned a long time ago that giving up is the last option. If it was important enough for you to fight for from the beginning, then it is just as important to see it all the way through. So what do you call limited?"

"Medical usage. Partnering perhaps with the medical outlets a few days a week…a few hours a day. And any expenses for such would be under the realm of the Lockwood Foundation. We'd begin with that. If and when we felt it right, we would then consider—and note I said *consider*—about the public having limited access. But that would be in the future. So I'm willing to talk to the medical team at the hospital and get some more information before I give the committee my answer. Fair enough?"

She wanted to shout to the rafters with relief but she knew that might be a little much for this man beside her. A hug? Best keep it professional…for all concerned. She nodded, not quite trusting her voice at the moment.

"Note that this moment is probably the one and only time you remain speechless." He was teasing her, but in a surprisingly gentle way.

"Enjoy it while you can." She came back to herself. "It won't last long or repeat itself."

He threw back his head and laughed and it sounded like an incredibly pleasing sound to her ears. She couldn't help but grin at his reaction. "That's the Tori I know." He stood and she joined him. "The rain has let up to a light mist so we best get you to your car while we can. I would offer you dinner but I have another meeting for this evening. We'll do a rain check. To seal the agreement after I've spoken to a couple of my advisors and such. Shake?" His hand was waiting.

Tori's was slower to make contact. When she did, his hand engulfed hers and there was that warmth from previous contacts. It could become addictive if one wasn't careful. It was capable and safe and too short. Tori had always been the careful one. Neither seemed inclined to make it brief.

"Thank you," she spoke into the growing silence. "This will mean so much to so many people needing help. And I can't help thinking how pleased your grandfather would be right now…or how proud."

They weren't shaking hands any longer. But their hands stayed joined. "I believe he just might be all of that. And it means a lot to you also, judging by the moisture in your eyes. I take it that it has made you happy also. But not for political reasons."

"You think you've gotten to know me so well?"

"I think you are a lady who lets few people inside that part of you where a human heart beats. You've had to be guarded for a long time, I'm guessing because you don't share much personally. But your heart—at least part of it—is set on making life better for those here in Destiny's River. Just like I imagine you did for years for your siblings. It wasn't chance you came here all those years ago. And it's much more that keeps you here. I look forward to gaining more insight into that heart of yours."

"Best be careful," she said without thinking. "That pretty lady you had lunch with earlier this week might have something to say about that." And she could have bitten her tongue. Where did those words come from?

His gaze narrowed and he finally released her hand. He didn't respond for a few moments. "True. She just might. And you reminded me that I'm going to be late for my meeting with her if I don't say goodbye now." He held his hand out but it was for the blanket and not her hand. They walked in silence to her car and he did not say goodbye but walked back to his house. Tori pulled away and kept from looking back in the mirror. She was kicking herself for saying what she did. She sounded like some childish, jealous female. Petty. After he had just agreed to what she wanted for so long. What must he think of her now?

☆

CADE LOCKWOOD WAS a man lost in his thoughts after he reached his bedroom. He had stood on the other side of his front door until he could hear the sound of her vehicle no longer as she departed the ranch. He was trying to determine what had happened in the couple of hours since she had arrived.

He sent a quick text to his dinner partner that he was running a bit late. Then he began changing his clothing after a quick shower. He had hoped the hot water would ease the tension in his body, but it hadn't. It was a feeling that had taken over his being the moment he kissed Tori Parker beside the pools. Just like his grandfather had kissed the love of his life. And he had wanted to shout to the man up above that he finally understood what he had meant. But he wasn't too clear on all of it himself, so he needed to slow it down. He had learned to be cautious. That all that glittered wasn't necessarily gold. He had been lied to before. He had been guilty of trying to put all women into the same category. And none had emerged to prove him wrong. Until there was Victoria Parker.

She challenged his preconceived notions. She met him head-on, toe to toe. Tori wasn't one to back down if she believed in the cause. He was beginning to see that could be due to the fact she, as the oldest, had to shoulder a lot of responsibility for the well-being of her siblings growing up. And she transferred that caring to those around her, many not even related to her. But they belonged to her adopted family of Destiny's River, and so they mattered. She championed their cause without hesitation.

There was one thing he could be sure of and that was the fact that Tori had been aware of his lunch with Selena, and it had brought a reaction from her. Why else would she have remarked upon it? Almost like she was jealous and wanted to let him know what she thought. But then she acted like she wanted to take back any and all of what she had said. As he thought over their conversation of the last couple of hours, and the kiss…and then the way they stood in the barn holding hands basically…well it made a slow smile move into place. There was something between them—he was certain of it. But what? He wasn't placing a label on it. Not yet.

As he retraced his steps down the stairs, and picked up his hat, fitting it on his head, his gaze caught that of his grandfather from the portrait on the wall. Was that the reason he had that hint of a secret smile on his face all this time? Did he have some way of looking into the future and seeing that his stubborn grandson would learn the secret one day as he had? He moved closer to look at the portrait of the man who had basically raised him. What he wouldn't give to have a conversation with him right in that moment.

"Victoria Parker, Granddad," he spoke to no one but the vision on the wall. "Did you know she'd show up one day and the springs would bring her? Just like they caught the heart of your lady long ago? She's one tough woman. She isn't used to letting people get too close and she likes to take care of herself without help from anyone else. Sound familiar? Do you know how this will end? You probably do…probably have a hand in it as usual. Well, I would appreciate it if you'd put in a good word for me with her if you can. I'm standing on quicksand here for the first time. But I do know that I don't want to be the next Lockwood who misses out on the love of their life. So there…I said it. Between you and me. I need you in my corner, Granddad. Because I have no idea what I'm doing next."

Cade paused in the doorway and looked back at the portrait. He could almost swear there was a hint of a wink. But that would be impossible. He closed the door behind him and whistled a tune as he made his way down the steps. It was one he heard the man in the portrait whistle many times. Cade knew why now.

Chapter Twelve

"CADE DID CALL, and we spoke this morning." Maggie imparted the information to Tori as they walked up the sidewalk toward the courthouse. The morning had come in with a light frost, and people had left sweaters behind in favor of jackets. Winter in Texas kept one moving between closets each day. The calendar spoke of late winter moving toward spring, but she felt winter was reserving a secret still to come. "You did it, girlfriend. You finally got Cade Lockwood to listen to you. And this town will be the better off for it."

"It was an effort by a lot of people, not just me. And I will be happy when all has been said and done and the springs are working for those who need their healing."

"But you are the one that took on that stubborn cowboy. To use a metaphor here…this time it was you who stayed the course for eight seconds and brought home the gold buckle. He and the doctors are already going over what is needed to bring the pools in question into compliance. And to make them user-friendly to the patients. He isn't letting the grass grow under his feet."

"Well, that's good. Keep me in the loop on what is going on." They had reached the top step and stood at the door.

"You haven't been talking with him?"

"Afraid I've been a bit busy with other things. There is always something else that needs attention on the list. And with that masquerade ball coming up that Leslie got passed by the council, I'm burning some late-night oil."

"Stop it. You're young and you need to be remembering that."

"What's that supposed to mean?" They had reached the door into her office suite and stepped inside.

"It means that you're still young and beautiful and single. So get out there and find Mr. Right and cozy up to something besides traffic charts and sewer surveys."

"Wise advice, Ms. Maggie. Hopefully our mayor will listen to it."

Tori cringed inside. She did not need to turn around to know that Cade Lockwood was standing behind her. When would she learn to keep private conversations just that? Keep them on the other side of her office and its closed door. She turned slowly and found herself just a couple feet away from the man. *Neutral smile, play the part.*

"Mr. Lockwood," she said. "I don't believe you're on my schedule today."

"True, Mayor Parker," he responded, his mimic of her greeting not lost on her. "But I did not think I needed to see you just to bring by your two pie plates that you left at the ranch for my crew. I told my housekeeper that I would drop them off."

Wallace spoke up. "And I put them in your office."

"And I need to get down the hall to my office," Maggie said. "Good to see you again, Cade. Look forward to our meeting on Thursday. Bye all!" Maggie abandoned her.

"Thank you for doing that. I appreciate it. Have a good day." She sailed around him and entered her office, closing the door behind her. *Rude? Okay, maybe. Coward? Yes.* She reminded herself that her new resolution was to keep Cade Lockwood far from her mind. Strictly business was the order of her days. Her list was long each day so she had plenty to keep her mind occupied. She sat down behind her desk, setting her coffee to the side, and began getting organized. The door opened and Wallace came in with the mail.

"Your appointment is here. It is a brief one with Dr. George from the hospital board. Then I expect the Ladies Guild to be early as usual. So if you finish with the good doctor early you can sail right into your next and maybe get out of here early today. Okay, don't give me that skeptical look of yours. A person can hope, can't one?"

"Yes, you just keep hoping, Wallace, for the both of us. Let's not keep the good doctor waiting."

And so the day was beginning and she had put the cowboy from her thoughts for a good five minutes. That was progress. She looked up with a smile at the door as her visitor entered. Then it froze.

"Good morning, Mayor Parker." The doctor extended his hand and they shook. "I had breakfast this morning with our friend here, Cade, and thought it would be a plus to bring him along to this meeting to bring you up to speed on a couple of things. You don't mind if he sits in with us?"

And what if she did? She smiled and graciously swept her hand toward the two empty chairs in front of her desk. "Of course not. Please make yourselves comfortable."

She managed to get through the preliminaries by keeping

most of her gaze on the doctor as he spoke. Very little attention landed on the cowboy who was dressed the part of a wealthy rancher that morning in a gray western-cut suit with vest, crisp white shirt and a black bolo tie with a silver etched concho with the Lockwood brand on it at the shirt's collar. His Stetson rested on the crossed knee of one leg. Maybe he had an 'engagement' next with his lady friend? And there went her attention to the last thing the doctor said.

"I'm sorry, Ian," she said. "Could you repeat that?"

"I was saying how helpful the Lockwood Foundation has been in getting things off the ground. It is amazing. Wait until you see what they have done and will still do out there and it…" His pager went off and he grimaced as he read the brief text.

"I'm sorry about the interruption, but I have an emergency consult," he said standing. "Perhaps Cade can fill in any details in my absence. Let's do lunch later this week, Tori. I'll call you." He was gone very quickly.

"Sorry."

She was forced to look over at the man still seated in front of her. "It couldn't be helped. But please don't think that you must stay. Our meeting was to be brief anyway."

"I take it that's my cue to leave. I know you're a very busy person." He stood and so did she.

"I'll take my leave. I know the way out." But he paused with his hand on the doorknob and looked at her. "You know I agree with Maggie on the advice she gave you."

"Advice?"

"The part about you being young and beautiful and

needing to get out and find Mr. Right. I won't repeat the part about traffic and sewers. But she is correct. There's more to life than this office, Victoria. But maybe you're afraid to venture outside it?"

"Afraid? I doubt I'm afraid. It's a question of priorities."

"So you don't consider a husband, children, home to be priorities?"

"Dreams don't always become realities, Mr. Lockwood. Some of us deal in the real world. My next appointment is here so I won't keep you."

He slid his hat onto his head and gave her one last look. "Realities can become priorities before you know it."

☆

"THIS IS A nice break in my day, but it might not be in yours," Matt said, shaking his head at his lunch companion. "I don't know if chaperoning a playdate for a bunch of six-year-olds is often on your social agenda. And the meal offered on the grill is hamburger sliders, chips, and one of Jillie's aunt's trays of cupcakes for dessert. You could be having better fare at Tillie's."

"No way," Cade replied, pushing back in the lawn chair and studying the group currently intent on redecorating the tree house in the corner of the yard. "Living dangerously on the back of a ton of mad bull might not be as challenging and not as much fun." He took a swig of the soda that Matt's daughter had presented him with on his arrival.

Matt laughed. "You might be right at that. But I promise we will have a grown-ups' lunch next week."

"It's a deal." Cade nodded. "You know, you're a good dad. It can't be easy being a full-time sheriff and a full-time single dad. Yet, you manage, and you've raised quite a young lady there."

"Thanks for the compliment on my daughter. But I cannot take full credit. I don't know what we would have done without Tori. I will always be grateful she wouldn't take no for an answer when she wanted me to bring Jillie and myself here to Destiny's River so she could help out with Jillie. It was my sis to the rescue as always."

"As always? Are you talking about her dedication to the town also?"

"Well, there is that too, I guess. But you probably aren't aware that the four of us—Tori, my sister Cassie, me, and my brother Rance—were raised in the foster system. Our mother died in a hit-and-run and we went to our grandmother. She eventually died of cancer, and we were placed into care. Tori always looked out for all of us. That's why when she aged out, she worked and saved money and went in search of a place we could know as home. She decided that Destiny's River was the place. And she was right. Each of us had the ability to go out and search out our own dreams with her help with money for schooling or whatever. I used to say that she was old long before she grew out of her teens. She fought battles of one kind or another. And she is still doing that wherever needed."

"Plus she bakes amazing desserts, runs a whole town, and can handle a horse pretty good."

"And according to my daughter she is the mostest awesome aunt in the entire universe."

Cade grinned. "That sums it up."

"Yes. And now why do I feel that you accepting this invitation was going to happen no matter what? This has something to do with Tori."

Cade sat forward in his chair, the empty bottle going on the table. He met Matt's inquiring gaze with a steady one on his part.

"You are a smart man. And an even better sheriff. What I can tell you is that your sister is good for this town. I believe that now. And anything else is something I'm not ready to share. But if that time comes, we'll talk again. In the meantime, how about getting those burgers done? I'm hungry."

☆

"REMIND ME THIS is for charity—a good cause. And keep reminding me over and over. And then remember that you promised you would never expect this from me again." Matt was trying to tie the bow tie for the third time and soon to be a fourth.

Tori gave an exasperated sigh and stepped up behind him. She batted his hands away from the material and began redoing the tie. "You are so helpless when it comes to dressing up. You spend too much time in uniform. Be still."

"This is ridiculous, Tori. Why did you go along with this idea? What happened to the fish fry we used to do? That made money."

"And that might still be done in the summer…when people want to be out on water and it isn't freezing. Stop griping and go along with it. You might have fun. Who knows?"

"You remember that you promised that if Lisa Johnson or Sara Masters…or Janet Nelson bid on me…you will jump in and bid. Right? You worked it out with Maggie, right? You give her the money that you get from me and all will be well."

She finished with the bow tie and patted it. "There…do not touch it again. And yes, I have your escape plan in place should one of those three bid on you."

"How about you? Anyone you want me to save you from?"

"I'm not like you; I don't take all of this to heart. People will bid and that is the whole point. We aren't arranging a marriage contract tonight. And it's dinner at the country club so no surprises. Look at it that you will get a great dinner out of it."

"Tori, you need to get ready," Leslie called from the hallway. "Your clothing is in the room next door. And, Matt, please don't forget your mask."

Tori followed Leslie into the dressing area next door. The door shut and Leslie couldn't contain her excitement. "This is going to be such a hit…I can feel it. And when you come out in the gown and headpiece we got on loan from my aunt in New Orleans…it will be the showstopper. Of course, I'm just so disappointed still that we couldn't get Cade Lockwood, the most eligible single of all, to participate. But he had to go to some meeting on the West Coast of all times. The show must go on."

Tori slowly shook her head. "Remember what I said when you brought up this idea of your aunt and her costumes. I won't be wearing anything risqué like you see during Mardi Gras in New Orleans…got it? G-rated."

"Of course not. No R-rated outfits. PG at the most," Leslie said, crossing her heart. "You will love it."

There was a knock on the door and Tori's hairdresser and the makeup artist that had been hired for the evening for all the women came in. Kristi was quick on reading the room and Tori's level of patience. "Everyone out now so we can prepare your showstopper, Leslie." She herded the woman from the room and shut and locked it.

"Thank you, Kristi." Tori smiled as the pair began unpacking their wares on the dressing table.

"Just relax," she said. "You're in our hands now and there's nothing to worry about."

Tori did just that. She sat back in the swivel chair and let the masters go to work. Closing her eyes, she settled in as Kristi put some soft music on the radio and they began her transformation.

"Okay, we'll touch up the makeup after we get you into the dress. And then again after we get your headpiece and mask on." Kristi and Lily the makeup artist began taking the gown out of its bag. It was a massive skirt and train, heavy with shimmering spangles and jewels in shades of scarlet reds fading into the black sequined top. The headpiece was an incredible mass of long black pheasant feathers jutting from the red sequined mask that covered her face to just above the mouth.

"You have your red and black stilettos on. Now step in carefully," the ladies instructed, holding both sides of the gown. They worked on securing the gown's zippers and ties.

Tori wasn't allowed to see her reflection until they were complete with her transformation. When they added the headpiece, Tori was thrown a bit off-balance. Luckily, the ladies quickly righted her.

"The dress weighs a ton with all the beading," Tori said. "And the headdress feels like someone set a brick weight on my head. The mask is itching. How am I supposed to act glamorous and mysterious in this?"

"Well, consider it mysterious in how you figure out the art of walking out on the runway without toppling over." Kristi grinned. "Let's put the scarlet lipstick on now and you'll be totally glamourized."

"Okay. Turn around slowly and look at the new version of you."

Tori did just that…especially the slow part. And then she froze.

She was quiet so long that Lily and Kristi finally spoke.

"Tori…what's wrong?"

"This is not G-rated. It would be hard pressed to say it's even PG," Tori began. "The skirt is slit so far up the side that there is no way I would dare sit down in it. And the top? What top? It's cut almost down to my navel in front. The off-shoulder top is not there for much support."

"Two positives." Kristi spoke up. "First is that you are stunning in it…you might not think so but it could have been made for your figure or vice versa. Second…with the mask and headpiece, most people if not all will not know who you are. So you can have some fun with that. Isn't that the point of the evening? Everyone is here to have fun and make some money for a good cause. So get out there and forget the comfort zone and have fun."

Have fun. Forget the comfort zone. Right. Tori had a feeling that she would regret volunteering. And she might never live the night down.

Chapter Thirteen

"MATT, IS THAT you?" Cade spoke in a quieter tone, not wanting to give anything away since no one was supposed to know who was in the auction. But remembered that Matt had burned his thumb on the grill doing the hamburgers and he noted the same red marks on the tuxedoed man standing a couple feet away, looking like he wanted to stay hidden behind the huge potted plant forever. Cade had moved over to stand a foot away from the man.

"What gave me away?" the man whispered back, keeping his attention on the rest of the room.

"Well, it might be the fact you look like you're trying to hide in a potted plant. Or it could be that I remember the red marks on the side of your thumb came from your mishap with the grill at your daughter's party. How are you holding up?"

"Besides actually trying to blend in with a plant for protection from the women around here, I guess I'm doing just great, Cade. Why aren't you participating?"

"I had a meeting today in San Francisco. I didn't think I'd get back in time, but we finished early and I just came in from the airport."

"You know, you could take my mask and blend in and do the auction."

"No thanks. I'll just be content with bidding. Who do you suggest I should put my money on…so to speak?"

"Well, the lady in the white feathers over there might be interesting. Or the one in blue. Or…hold on! Who is that?"

Cade swung his gaze in the direction Matt was looking and he had to do a double take. "Talk about the lady in red. Who in the world is that?"

Matt shook his head. "I don't know but I bet all the men are rushing to the nearest ATM and making transfers."

"Which is your sister?"

"Sorry, I have no idea. She was dressed in her costume after I came out here to scope things out. Looks like the vision in red and black has gone backstage already. It was just a tease to get the bidders ready. And I see that Leslie is motioning to me. So last chance to take my place, friend?"

Cade shook his head with a grin in the man's direction. "Wouldn't deprive you of such an honor. You are making a great sacrifice for the cause."

Matt turned and gave an impression of someone walking to the gallows.

The music started and the lights dimmed. A spotlight would pick up the person up for auction as they came out on stage, made their walk, and then turned for the bidding to begin. Cade edged closer to the end of the runway in hopes he would be able to recognize the woman he planned to bid on. He had to hope that something would tell him which was Tori.

The lady in white came out first. The bidding was spirited for the first one. Then one of the men came out. The ladies did not hold back. Luckily for the charity, the crowd was getting into the fun. By the fourth one to come out, which was Matt, they had broken a thousand-dollar ceiling with the last bid. It was clear that three ladies were dead serious in outbidding each other. Cade caught Matt's pleading look behind his mask and only grinned bigger in response. One woman triumphed and it was clear that Matt hadn't counted on her winning.

The final bid of the evening was the lady in red as she had come to be known in his mind. The music became pure Cajun slow jazz and the lady began her walk down the runway. And she was working it like no other. The cheering and clapping seemed to entice her to really sell it in the outfit that suited a pair of knockout long legs and a good amount of other areas of skin that flashed and sparkled as she moved. She was moving toward where he stood and he found there was something about her that held his attention. Then her gaze found his interested one and she seemed to turn away and then stop. A long length of leg played with the high split in the skirt and she gave a come-hither pose over her shoulder, a slow wink through the sequined mask, and then a scarlet kiss was blown in his direction. The crowd roared and then with a toss of her head, she made her way back to the center of the stage. The emcee, which was Leslie, opened the bidding and it was fast and furious.

The high bid was twelve hundred. Cade had held back as others outbid each other. It rose to fifteen hundred and it looked like one of the doctors from the local hospital just might win the lady. Cade nodded. The doctor lasted through two more bids and then Cade decided to end it all.

"Ten thousand dollars." Silence in the room.

Leslie looked like she might pass out. But she quickly recovered and there being no one else who chose to outbid him, she shouted *sold.* Thunderous applause broke out. Cade walked over to the steps where each person had been handed over to the person who bid on them. He watched the sparkling vision walk toward him. He raised his hand to help her down the steps. Once her hand was in his, he grinned. He had gotten it right.

"I seem to be the most envied man here tonight. Do you have a particular name or should I just call you my lady in red?"

"Do you plan to keep this up all evening? How did you figure it out?"

He grinned. "At the springs, just before you made that graceful entrance into the pool…I noticed a tiny perfect little butterfly on the back of your ankle. The same ankle that you were so helpful to show to me when you did your sexy turn in front of me on the runway."

"That's cheating."

"Is it? Then why hadn't I bid on anyone before you came out? I think I would recognize those amazing eyes even with a mask and those scarlet lips…well, no one can smile the way you can. Should I go on?"

"No. Thank you for your contribution tonight. The charity fund will be able to be even more helpful this year."

"Will you be wearing this outfit when we dine out?"

"Absolutely not."

"Too bad. I think you should wear feathers more often and who knew our mayor had such legs?"

"You are getting way too much enjoyment out of my

public embarrassment."

"Admit it, you were having some fun up there on that runway."

"The only thing I admit to right now is that my feet have moved beyond the unbearable pain stage. How some women can wear these silly high heels longer than two minutes is beyond me. So, beware of a woman experiencing great pain in her feet. Nothing is funny at this point."

"I understand. Come with me." He didn't wait for her response but had control of her hand in his and she tried to keep up.

He paused long enough to say something to one of the catering staff and then he continued on down a hallway to a quiet alcove that was set back into an atrium area.

"Sit down," he instructed. There was a bench that sat in the area.

"I warn you that if I sit now, I may not get back up again."

"That's a chance we'll take." The catering person appeared and handed a basket to him and then returned to the ballroom.

Cade sat down on the bench then.

"I'm not getting fresh with you," he said as a preamble to his next move. He reached down and drew one leg over to rest her foot on his knee. Then he made short work of taking off the offending shoe and placing it on the floor. From the basket, he withdrew a towel.

"This might be a little warmer than you like. Just let me know." He slowly wrapped the heated towel around her foot. "Too warm?"

"No, I like it warmer like that. How did you know to do this? Your friend must wear high heels like that."

"She does. And I watched her do this on occasion." He began to kneed beneath the arch of her foot. The warmth of the towel and his expert touch worked their magic.

"You are surprising to say the least," she said. "A man with many talents. But you didn't have to do this."

Cade shook his head. "Other foot." He began the same work on the new foot.

"You don't like it when someone does something unexpected for you…maybe tries to help you out. I first thought it was just me that you didn't like helping you out. But then I realized that it's others, too. You don't like giving over any of your control to anyone else. You know sometimes it's good to have someone to share the load with. It doesn't mean you aren't strong enough. Sometimes it takes a lot of guts to admit that two heads are better than one."

"More of your armchair psychology?"

"Just experience."

"Guess I sounded like a witch the last few minutes." She relented. "I'm sorry. I could blame it on being tired. Or my feet hurting."

"You could. Give yourself a break. And that leads to the dinner part of this evening. How about we just choose to enjoy a nice evening, free food, good company. And you can leave the feathers and the shoes at home."

"Agreed. And now I'm going to go change out of this heavy outfit and toss the shoes in a dumpster."

"That's a shame. You could wear them on special occasions. For special people…or a special person. Just a suggestion." The grin gave him away.

She took possession of her foot again. Tori stood but preferred to stay in her stocking feet.

"Time for Cinderella to leave this ball."

"That makes me Prince Charming?" He stood.

"You might be."

"I'll do my best to earn the title."

"Good night and thank you again for your contribution...and the best foot rub ever."

☆

"CADE LOCKWOOD BID more money for you than ever before in any event we have hosted, he then gave you a foot rub, and not to mention the work crew he sent to your house and putting you on the back of a horse that has been your dream forever... Oh and did I forget to add that he is opening the warm springs after you persuaded him? I would say that the man just might be interested in *you*. And you are oblivious."

"Maggie...he isn't interested. I told you he has a mysterious model-looking woman he's obviously dating. I don't know what he is interested in being nice to me for, but he is up to something."

"Did you ask him about this girlfriend? None of the rest of us have seen her."

"Matt has and he was instantly a fan."

"Okay...plain talk. Put this supposed girlfriend aside. Would you be interested?"

"Reality check." Tori pushed aside the last of her glass of

tea. "Our worlds are vastly different. Our lives, our pasts...not even close. So let it go."

"You're having dinner tonight, right?"

"Only because he bid high enough. But yes, we will dine tonight and that's all."

"Then go out with a bang. Wear that cute little black outfit that has been hibernating in the back of your closet for far too long. Don't talk business. Have a *real* conversation. Enjoy the company. At midnight, you can return to your little inn, to your cat, and then wake up and go to your mayor job again."

"Maggie, you are a hopeless romantic."

"Never hopeless, just always hopeful. It's *your* turn, you know. Go out and find something *you* deserve—for yourself, no one else. You've raised your siblings. They are all productive and happy members of society. And they would each say the same thing I'm saying to you right now."

Something I deserve. The words replayed in her head as she dressed for dinner later that evening. What did she deserve? In her mind, she had simply done what was needed. She was the oldest, and yet, she was just thirteen when their world changed, and they entered the system. But she had known that childhood was gone, and she did not waste time mourning it. Instead, she was determined to keep them all together, made sure they each had a fair chance to grow up as naturally as they could in the system without anyone who cared about them. And she had vowed that one day, there would be a place called home that all of them would know, where they belonged for the rest of their lives.

So strike the word *deserve*. Maybe replace it with *earned.*

She hadn't had an easy road, but she had navigated it. Just as so many others had to do. If she was taking what she earned that evening, then it would be a free dinner, wearing a dressy outfit she had also earned the money to buy, and she would spend some time with another human, not a stack of papers and charts.

It had been three days since the auction. Tonight was the 'romantic candlelight dinner' that the winning bidder was due. She would fulfill her part of the deal. And she eyed the black dress that Maggie had said she should wear. It had hung on the door for the last two days…while she debated what to wear. Finally, she had decided to follow part of Maggie's advice. She'd wear the dress. But the rest of her advice involving going after the man…well, that would be the part she ignored.

She had just finished applying the last dab of perfume when the doorbell rang. Her heart suddenly sped up. *Calm down. It's just dinner and then back home. He is just a business associate.*

Maggie had been right on her suggestion of the little black dress if the look on Cade Lockwood's face was any indication. His gaze made a slow scan of her and her outfit and it came back to meet her gaze.

"I'm beginning to think this might be even better than those feathers. You look beautiful. And far more relaxed."

Relaxed? No way. Not when a handsome cowboy was standing on her doorstep calling her beautiful and looking at her the way she read about in those romance novels her sister would buy. Trouble might be ahead.

"Shall we go?" Cade's words brought her back to reality.

He took her evening coat from her and held it while she slipped it on. It was one of the reasons she had bought the outfit. The dress was classy and the matching coat was cut with a flair to it and tiny pearl buttons from the neck to the waist. She had braided her hair back into a French knot with a black ribbon intertwined. Tiny pearls shone in her earlobes. *Classy* was what she had hoped for.

"Did you trade in your truck?" She made the comment when she saw the shiny black limo at the end of the sidewalk. The chauffeur held open the door for them.

"Can't win the title of Prince Charming if I pick up Cinderella in a truck, can I?"

"You have a competitive streak in you. Anyone ever tell you that?"

"A few rodeo cowboys. And now you."

The ride in the limo was interesting. It was the first time she had ever ridden in one. Glancing at the man beside her, she noted he seemed to be quite at ease. He looked like a man accustomed to limo rides and then he could also look like a cowboy who loved his truck. *Nice mixture.*

The country club was on the outskirts of town, overlooking the lake that was formed when they placed a dam across the lower part of the river. Floor-to-ceiling windows gave a view of lights twinkling through the trees on the far shore. The private community was where the richer inhabitants had built their homes…the doctors and lawyers and rich tourists looking for that 'little country place' for vacations.

Their table was set in a private dining area with white linen, fine china, and candlelight. A long-stemmed red rose lay across her place setting. The waiter pushed in her chair once she had removed her coat and sat down.

A bottle of champagne was opened and sat chilling in a bucket next to the table. The waiter poured each of them a glass and then discreetly disappeared.

"Leslie has outdone herself. When she said a fine dining candlelight experience, she wasn't kidding."

"Too much for your taste?" Cade asked.

"It's nice on very special occasions, I suppose. Otherwise, I could get just as excited with a picnic basket beside a pond. It really depends on the person you're sharing it with... That's what would make it special in my mind."

"Duly noted."

"Why are you smiling like that? Something funny in what I said?"

"I was just reflecting over the time I have known you and how many layers of Victoria Parker I have learned about. And they keep appearing. Which one is the definitive you? Are they all part of the real you?"

"What do you mean?"

"Are you the professional buttoned-up mayor? Or the Mardi Gras vixen in red? The woman who wears jeans and has great joy over a horseback ride? The woman who gives her all and her life to raise her siblings and still looks out for them?"

"You make me sound like a mystery. I'm not. I'm all of those when I need to be. If you ask which I enjoy the most? Then that's easy. I love my family, and they come first always. If I could wear jeans every day in the mayor's office, then I would. If being a vixen as you call it gets money for children in need, then bring on the feathers. I am just *me.*

Nothing special."

"That is the most ridiculous thing I have heard from you. Believe me, before I met you...when you were just this interloper who had come to town a few years ago and dared to run for mayor, I might have bought into that description you just gave. But now, I know better. You *are* special, Victoria Parker. I guarantee that. And it's time you had your eyes opened to the fact." He raised his glass for a toast. She did the same.

"To you and all that you are." His gaze matched the tone of his words, and she felt a surge from the tips of her toes to the top of her head. Was it his look or was it the champagne?

"Do you have your dancing shoes on tonight?"

His question threw her for a moment. It was such a change of subject.

"I like to dance but I'm very rusty. It's been a while."

"Then let's get you back in practice." He stood and held out his hand.

The quintet had begun when they arrived and there were three or four couples already on the dance floor. He drew her hand in his and then swung her around to end up against his solid chest. Through a two-step, fox trot, salsa, waltz...they danced each one. He led and she followed. To her amazement, their steps matched without much thought. She had forgotten what fun it was to dance with a partner who enjoyed it as much as she did.

Finally, he led her back to the table. Menus appeared and they ordered. Another glass of champagne was poured.

"I'm thinking this might be my last glass," she said. "I'm not used to it."

He motioned to the waiter. "We'd like two glasses of iced tea, please. And you can keep those coming."

The waiter smiled and left them.

"You didn't have to order tea for yourself. I don't mind being the lightweight around here."

"I prefer a clear head myself."

"You know a lot about me but what about you? Why don't you still rodeo?"

"I have a ranch that needs me present. And rodeo is a younger man's sport now. I have a drawer full of buckles and trophies on shelves. I also have quite a few bones patched together. And a crooked nose as you pointed out when we first met. It was fun during that first part of my life, but life on the road gets old and fast. And as my grandfather grew older, I realized that he had hopes that he could turn over the running of the ranch to me. I needed to learn all I could while I had him as my teacher."

"All those buckle bunnies following you around and none of them managed to land you?"

"I'm not a choir boy. But none of them ever got as far as my heart. None that I couldn't forget about their names the next day. Sorry if that answer was a bit rough. But I always was able to walk away without a backward thought. That had to be a sign, I figured."

"It was an honest answer. That's refreshing. And now you are in the next phase of your life…gentleman rancher? And you still haven't settled down."

"No, but there is always hope. I realize that."

"I see. Hope as in the woman I saw you with? Thinking of finally settling down?"

"I might be thinking of settling down, but the lady is still a question mark. And it certainly would not be Selena. Marrying your half-sister isn't exactly where it's at for me."

Silence. All manner of words had rushed to her brain when the door had been opened to the subject of "that other female," but none were relevant at that moment. Because there was no other woman—at least not one who posed an issue that had been built up in her brain. Since she witnessed the hug and cheek kiss. She had prepared herself for that one. But somehow the term *half-sister* had just punctured that balloon in her mind.

"I see. You have a sibling named Selena. But she doesn't live here...at least I guess not? I haven't heard too much mention of her."

He shook his head. "No and that is the way it has been since she and her mother moved to Dallas when she was in middle school. Her mother and my father had a fling, for want of a better word, that lasted about six months. When it became evident that he wasn't going to toss off my mother, his wife, for her when she turned up pregnant, she opted to top off her bank account and leave. Selena and I saw each other on holidays when she could come back to the ranch per the visitation clause that went along with the money her mother received from my father. And then when she was old enough to make her own decisions and her mother had moved on to greener pastures with a banker in New York, she spent more time with my grandfather and me on the ranch. When he died, he left her land and funds to start her own dream, which was a winery and vineyard. Which she turned out to be quite good at. Now we see each other when we can, which isn't all that often. And there you have the story of the mystery woman in my life. The only one there is, for the record."

It was time to turn her attention to the food and not his personal life or the fact he was thinking of settling down with the right person. He just hadn't found that person evidently. Tori's appetite seemed to have fled.

The dessert course came and he shook his head after looking at the menu.

"You don't see what you want?" she asked.

"I know what I want; it's not on this menu."

"What would that be?"

"Well, I know this woman who makes the most delicious pecan pie. That would be the fitting end to this meal."

She shook her head. "You sound a lot like my brother. I tell him to just come out and tell me what he wants. Things would go a lot faster."

"Does that advice go for most things? Just tell you straight out what I, or he, wants? Cut to the chase so to speak?"

Why did that sound like a trick question? She should back off. But then she didn't take her own advice sometimes.

"I have a fresh pecan pie at home. I can offer you a slice with a cup of coffee if you would prefer that."

"What are we still sitting here for?" He smiled and she would swear it had a triumphant upturn to it.

☆

"YOUR INN IS quite welcoming. Everything looks like the

perfect country accommodation. I've heard it's quite popular." He made the remark while she plated the slices of pie and poured the coffee. She sat them on the small kitchen dining table. He took the seat she indicated.

"Thank you. I couldn't manage without my housekeeper-slash-major domo Miss Minnie. She and her son keep the place running, the tenants taken care of, and the gardens filled with beauty. They came here about ten years ago and ended up staying on to help me expand this business. They are extended family, so to speak."

"And it's also your home. It has that feel to it…warmth, welcoming, a good place to sit a spell in one of those rockers on the porch and watch the sunsets."

Cade was pleased to see that his words brought a soft smile to her face and a gleam to those blue eyes.

"That was my dream when I settled here. I added the individual little houses with mini kitchens around the garden and now the main house here is just the family home. We do serve dinners on Sunday evenings and breakfast on certain mornings buffet-style in the glassed-in sunroom for the guests," Tori said. "Sorry but this isn't as fancy as our earlier meal."

"It's better." He stated that just before taking a bite of pie. Then there was another.

It wasn't long before there were just a few crumbs left on his plate.

"Where did you learn to bake like this?"

"I watched and listened to my grandmother. She was a great cook. Everything from scratch. And after we ended up in foster care, I realized that I could bake cookies and cakes for others and they would pay me. That was money I could save for when we would all need a place to call home. As I grew older, I found I could sell to others in the community and expanded my menu items."

"Well you can certainly cook. I was most impressed the night Matt brought me to dinner even though I wasn't exactly welcome. You fed me and didn't try to poison me."

"You were lucky. I couldn't do it with the sheriff present."

There was a stretch of silence after the laughter subsided. She stood and began to clear the dishes.

"Don't you hate awkward moments like this?" He had stood up and was watching her.

His question seemed to surprise her. "Awkward?"

"I am taking your advice. State your case and get it over with, you said. Don't waste time. You never know how precious little of it there might be. So here goes." He took the coffee mug from her hand and set it in the sink. Then he placed his hands on either side of her so that she was more or less a captive audience with the cabinet behind her. Was it his heart that was beating so loudly?

"We could beat around this subject for a while, but time would be wasted. I'll put it plain and simple. I like you Victoria Parker. I also like Tori Parker. You keep me on my toes and call me out when I need it. You can be maddening. You can also be pretty damn amazing…always surprising me. You keep me off-kilter and no one has managed to do that."

"Is that all?"

"And there is this." His hands slid around her waist and brought her up against him as his head lowered and his mouth claimed hers in a much different kiss than the first one. He was searching, exploring, drawing her into his kisses. It was natural that somehow her hands found their way over the broad shoulders and locked behind his head. As the kiss deepened, the heat coursed through both their bodies, sending nerve ends rioting and pulses out of control. A fire had begun deep within and it was threatening to blaze out of control. A faint bell began in the back of his mind and it wouldn't stop. There was a slight shift in the pressure on his lips and then he felt a soft groan escape him and the bell gained clarity. It was a phone. And the moment fractured like fragile glass.

Cade raised his head and sought control of his breathing. He muttered something and jerked the cell from his pocket. He took a step back as he answered with a curt hello.

The moment gave Tori time to slip away and gather her wits about her. The call ended and he turned to her.

"I need to get to the ranch. We have a problem with a mare that is foaling. The vet is on the way."

"I totally understand. It's late and I do have an early meeting."

"I hate that…"

"You probably need to hurry. And we will blame this on the champagne. Good night, Cade."

"This is something we will discuss again. But I'll leave now. Sweet dreams, Tori."

Chapter Fourteen

"HE KISSED YOU and then he left. And you don't plan to see him again. Are you crazy?"

Trust her sister to cut to the chase. Tori had been surprised to find her on her doorstep early that next morning. It wasn't often her sister, Cassie, could get away from her assignment but when she could, it was a great surprise. Except her highly trained interrogator experience wasn't fun to be on the receiving end of. Cassie had easily found out why there were telltale signs of a night spent tossing and turning and tears even being shed.

"No, I have my senses. That's why I don't intend to have this go any further. It's better to end it before it begins. It has catastrophe written all over it. I'm not the type of woman who would fit into the life of a Lockwood. I don't need that drama in my life."

Cassie sat looking at her sister for a moment or two. "You don't need drama. What type of BS is that? Last I looked, life is always full of drama of one kind or another. Our lives are perfect examples of that. From the time we were little kids up until and including today. You always taught us that we were never to count ourselves out against anyone else who might have more or be more or whatever. We needed to realize that it was what was inside a person that counted the most. And you have a multimillionaire gorgeous cowboy obviously interested in you if he drops thousands of dollars to have dinner with you when he could have just as easily written a check and dropped it in the mail if he wanted to contribute. He fixed the gutter issue on your home without expecting anything for it. Yet you have already counted yourself out where he is concerned.

"And to have him do the things he has done and say the things he has said…and you just want to tell him to take a hike because you are afraid of what *might* happen? Where is my tough big sister and what have you done to her?"

"I'm right here. Now let's order some lunch. Our brother probably got held up and I do have to make a dent in putting together a new budget. What looks good to you on the menu?"

Cassie did not respond to the question. Tori looked up from her menu. "I thought you were on a limited schedule today also. We need to order. What interests you?" Cassie wasn't looking at her.

Her attention was on something behind her. "I would say I want one of those, but I believe he's taken."

"He? What are you talking about?" About that time, Matt appeared beside the table. Tori looked up at him and then at her sister. "Are you talking about Matt?"

"It's a good topic if you are." Matt spoke up, drawing out a chair. "Let me make introductions."

"No need," Cassie said, the smile on her face almost gleeful as she raised her hand. That's when another person stepped around from behind Tori and shook hands with her sister. "I believe you must be Cade Lockwood. I'm Cassandra

Parker. Cassie to most."

"I ran into this fellow over at the courthouse and invited him along. Hope you ladies don't mind?" Matt was too cheerful as he settled into his chair. Tori wasn't in the mood for whatever he was up to. Cassie was still smiling as she shook hands with the man still standing.

"I think this is great. I've heard so much about you from my siblings. Do sit and join us."

"Good afternoon, Mayor." Cade finally acknowledged her presence. "I hope I'm not interrupting a family get-together."

"Good afternoon," she responded, aware they were drawing attention from the other diners. "Do sit down."

"We were just about to order, Matthew. I have to get back to the office soon."

"Matthew," the sheriff said with a grin. "That means I have done something wrong and my big sister is warning me to behave. But I am starving first and foremost. Let's place our orders so the mayor can get back to work."

Tori felt like she might as well not even be at the table. Between the three of them, they soon had a conversation going like old friends. Cassie was being especially friendly to Cade and Tori recognized what she was doing. She was quite skilled in getting people to open up and draw them out and before they knew it, she would have gotten the information she wanted. Tori wasn't in the mood. Both her siblings needed to take a step back. The food came and she ate hers, making as few comments as necessary.

"Well, I must leave. Cassie, you have the key to my house, in case Minnie is out doing errands. So make yourself at home as usual and I will try to get back early. Matt, do remember to stop by Dorinda's and pick up the flour tortillas she's making for tonight."

"Cade's doing that on his way into town."

"Yes, I pass right by Dorinda's little bakery. It's the only contribution Matt would let me make toward this little birthday celebration for Jillie." Cade supplied the missing information for Tori.

"I didn't realize that you knew Jillie," was all she managed to respond with.

"Cade helped me corral the group of seven-year-olds last week that came over for a playdate in the backyard. He came in handy with the grill when the chef had a little mishap and burnt his thumb instead of a burger," Matt added with a laugh. "He and Jillie became fast friends. She invited him to join us."

"I see." Tori needed some air. And she needed her family to realize that whatever they were up to, it wasn't going to work. Most of all, Cade Lockwood needed to stay away. But she would deal with all of that later. She stood up. "Then I will leave you all to enjoy the rest of your lunch."

She didn't wait around for their responses. Tossing a wave at Tillie, she kept a smile on her face until she was outside and then she marched back to her office in record time. She went straight through to her office and then she stopped.

Wallace was right behind her. "You didn't give me time to tell you that you had a special delivery while you were out. I sat them in here so people would stop making excuses to come by and look in to see what had arrived for you from the florist. I must say that LaVernia outdid herself on this display."

"Display is right. What in the world?" She moved over to where her desk was almost hidden by the massive arrangement of all her favorite flowers...roses in different shades of pink, tall glads in a bright fuchsia, baby's breath and greenery and even some little white button mums appearing amongst the larger flowers. A white card was almost hidden by the huge pink bow. She opened the envelope and drew out the card. One word...*Cade.* No other sentiment was added, but the flowers spoke it for him. What was he thinking to have this delivered to her office? It would be the talk of the town within the hour if it wasn't already.

First, he shows up at lunch in the crowded café and now he sends a massive number of roses to the courthouse. The man clearly doesn't care about appearances. How easily people can and would get the wrong idea.

"Should I move them over to the table?" Wallace stepped around her and stood waiting beside her desk.

"Please do. I need to be able to see my desk so I can work at it." She made sure that the card went inside her bag. But the sender had already been ferreted out from the florist, she was sure. Nothing was kept a secret for long in Destiny's River.

"Someone has an admirer," gushed Maggie as she sailed into the office. Wallace left them to it after moving the arrangement, closing the door behind him. "Pink roses and they smell heavenly."

"I suppose it is already going to be front page in the newspaper?" Tori made the remark as she sat down behind her desk.

"If it isn't today, it will be tomorrow." Maggie grinned. "I have to be in court in five minutes, but I just had to come see what everyone downstairs was whispering about. I'd say the man just sent you a message. That trip you both took was my idea. Just remember that when you send out the wedding invites." She made for the door before Tori had a chance to aim something in her direction.

What was the man up to? Was this the usual way he treated his women? Fancy dinner, an earth-shaking kiss, and then flowers the next day? Well, he'd wasted his money and time. If he gave the townspeople something to talk about that morning, then she could help in the afternoon.

"Wallace," she spoke into the intercom. "Please step in."

He wasted little time. "Yes, Mayor?"

"I would like you to deliver these flowers someplace for me."

"Your home? I'd be happy to do so."

"No, not my home. I think the lovely people at the nursing home deserve to enjoy them. It will brighten the day. Please take them over there with my best wishes for a wonderful day."

"You are sending them away…to the nursing home? That is such a touching gesture, Mayor. I will do it right now." The flowers were on the move and out of her office.

Tori smiled to herself. Let that bit of news get around town and right to Cade Lockwood. It would be one bright topic in the evening ahead.

☆

JILLIE'S BIRTHDAY WOULD be celebrated with her family at the dinner that Tori always prepared for her. She would do it up 'fancy-style' as the child liked to call it. Then they would have a kids' party on Saturday afternoon. The only problem was that rain had been forecast for part of the day and Tori was worried about what the backyard would look like after a group of children tried playing in wet grass and mud. But she would come up with plan B before then.

Tori hurried home, realizing she was already running behind schedule. Darn building inspectors wouldn't stop talking about budget items they just had to have. She left them sorting it out and literally ran to her car. The smell of food cooking met her as she ran through the kitchen door.

"Is the casserole ready for the oven? Beans on?"

Cassie was in the center of the kitchen, apron on, and nodding. "Casserole, check. Beans check. Dining room table is set. I'm working on the salad now. Matt dropped off the extra bag of ice in the freezer and has gone home to help the birthday girl get ready."

"Good, I'll run up and change and get back down here to finish up the cake." She breezed through the kitchen, gave a swift hug of thanks to her sister, ran through the dining room checking its bright decor out and then up the stairs to her bedroom for a quick shower and change.

Applying the last of her makeup, she had scanned her closet, dismissing what her original outfit was to be and coming up with another one. She wasn't making the change because of a change in the guest list, she told herself. But just because she felt a need to be an even more festive hostess. Jillie had decreed that she wanted her favorite Mexican food for her birthday, so they had decorated the dining room in festive colors from the tablecloth to the napkins, stoneware in bright colors, papier-mâché flowers suspended on gaily colored ribbons from the ceiling, and music to match the event playing. Jillie would have her fiesta dinner.

Tori had bought a bright blue peasant blouse with an off-the-shoulder ruffle flounce at the neckline. The skirt was cut with a generous flare of panels of multi-colors. Her hair she let hang down and tucked a bright pink flower behind her ear. That was the best the hostess could do with a cake still waiting for a final touch-up. She ran down the stairs and stopped in the doorway of the kitchen. Cassie was laughing at something the tall man with his back to Tori had just said. *Talk about a party downer.* Tori's smile dimmed. The pair turned as they realized someone else had come into the room.

"Our guest came to help."

"Please." He smiled at her sister. "I'm here to work and help, not as a guest. Just tell me what to do." Then he just had to add, "And not necessarily where to go." That was clearly aimed at her. The smile came back to her face. *Fun evening ahead.*

She headed to the far cabinet and began to assemble the decorations she would add to the cake, which had already been baked and iced and was ready to be completed. Tori blocked out the other two in the kitchen and began her work. Bright-colored trim and lots of roses per Jillie's request, and then the writing: *'Happy 8th Birthday, Jellybean.'*

"That is some cake," came the praise from the man who had been standing a few feet away so as not to distract her.

"But Jilliebean?"

"That has been the nickname for Jillie since she was born," Cassie responded. "Her aunt Tori gave it to her and the family followed suit."

"I see," Cade said with a smile. "It suits her."

"Well, I'm going to get ready upstairs. Matt will let us know when they're getting close."

Tori added the last rose and stepped back. She was pleased.

"Those bright roses are a nice touch."

He was alluding to other roses and they both knew it. She might as well get it over with while they had the kitchen to themselves. She turned to face him.

"Nice touch? Let's talk about the roses that arrived in my office and have become the talk of this town. Why would you do something so outrageous?"

"Was that wrong of me? I thought most women liked flowers and you did mention that roses where your favorite. Did I get that wrong?"

"Roses are my favorite. But when you send such an outrageous number that leads to all sorts of speculation from others, and you know it. Why did you do it?"

"Well, I saw the flower shop and I thought of you, so I wanted to let you know that you were being thought about. I would have stopped by and delivered them myself but I didn't think that would be a good idea since you never seemed to like me just dropping in to your office. I was trying to not upset you."

"Well, you managed to do it. Because now we are the talk of the town. And I don't like being part of the daily gossip."

"I'm not sure what the problem is exactly now since you made it clear you didn't want them around and I understand they did brighten the day for a lot of people at the nursing home. Nice gesture on your part. But then that only stoked the gossips more who think we might be having a lover's tiff or something."

"Lover's tiff? Are you crazy? We are not lovers, and I dare anyone to say that around me."

He had the audacity to smile. And he moved closer, one hand reaching out and carefully removing the icing knife from her hand and placing it in the sink. "I think it is better our conversations do not have sharp objects around them. This also isn't the place for this discussion. But I am sorry that I upset you by what I did to try and make you smile by sending your favorite flowers. I'm not versed in flowers as I don't usually send a lot of them. But I was thinking about you, so I did it on the spur of the moment. I have learned a lesson. Now can we agree to try to make a truce for Jillie's party?"

Tori hated it when he was right. And something tried to tug at her heartstrings, which she wasn't used to dealing with. But it was Jillie's evening, and they could behave like adults for a few hours, right?

"Agreed."

"Now I have a couple of calls to make so I'll step into the living room and leave the master chef to her kitchen."

Cassie came down the back stairs into the kitchen. She looked around and then gave a deep sigh in her sister's direction. "You didn't run him off while I was gone did you?"

"No, I did not. We agreed to try and behave like adults this evening for the sake of the party. He's gone to make a couple of calls." She began pulling out other platters and pans from beneath the cabinet.

"I didn't check but he did remember the tortillas, right?"

"Yes, Tori. He arrived with them, and they are in the warmer. And just in case you want to know...I happen to like him. You do too. So get off your stubborn high horse and do something about it."

"This is not a discussion we are having now. Let it alone."

"It's not that. It's the fact that you sabotage every relationship that might look promising. You have for years. For some reason, you won't let go and be like the rest of us. We fall in love...we lose out. It hurts but someone, remarkably like you, always told us not to quit. Fight for what we want. We deserved it. Well, here is a newsflash for you. *You* deserve it now. This is your time. We three are grown up and have our own lives to deal with. So take your own advice and deal with it. And that will be the last I will say on the subject. I'll make the cake table ready for your creation." She left Tori alone.

Why couldn't people just understand? But then she answered her own question with another. How could they understand when she didn't herself? Cade Lockwood had been a major surprise from the beginning. They had been oil and water. Then something had happened on their trip to view the springs, and now they looked at each other like two people who might or might not like each other. But he had to go and kiss her, not once but twice. And she didn't like the feeling of being out of control. That had been her strength all her life, it had seemed. She was the problem-solver. But her heart was betraying her over her brain. She needed to hang on to her mind for protection.

Again, she heard the shared laughter coming from the dining room. Why couldn't she trust what Cassie was saying? And why didn't she trust him?

Because you are afraid. For the first time ever, you are afraid of losing something very vital...your heart.

Chapter Fifteen

JILLIE WAS HAPPY. From the moment the long limo had pulled up to the front of Tori's house, and they had stood on the porch to watch its arrival, the child had been treated like royalty. Tori had been informed by Cassie that the limo was Cade's gift to her. Tori might have known. And she had stepped out like a princess in her purple velvet outfit and a sparkling tiara on her head. Yet another member of her family had succumbed to the smiling cowboy accepting one of Jillie's special hugs. Seemed she was the only member of the family, besides her other brother, who was on special assignment and couldn't come for her birthday, who had not given the seal of approval.

"I hope all my friends saw me. They watched when I got picked up after school in a real limo. No one else has even been in one. Wasn't it a great surprise?" She was gushing and Tori kept on smiling and agreeing. The man had definitely made an impression.

Jillie sat in the guest of honor chair at the head of the table. The food covered the length of it and everyone found room for second helpings. She noted Cade even had a third go at the casserole. She had to smile at that.

Gifts came next. Jillie loved each and every one and had to bestow hugs around the table. Matt just shook his head.

"No wonder my daughter is so spoiled with aunts like the pair of you. You have spoilt her since the day she was born."

"That's right," Cassie spoke up. "And you are just jealous because we don't throw you a party too."

"We did," Tori corrected. "We did it twice since he became sheriff and each time he had to be called away and missed his own dinner. So, we gave up."

"Yes." He nodded. "But somehow there was always a piece of birthday cake waiting for me in the kitchen cabinet when I finally got back. My big sis would never own up to it, but I know she made sure I was reminded it was my day. Funny how you always managed to do that since we were old enough to realize what a birthday was. Thanks." And he smiled across at Tori with a lot of love, and she had suddenly remembered she had to do something in the kitchen. She left for a moment.

She dabbed at her eyes, trying not to smear her makeup. The door squeaked open and she knew it was probably Cassie. A Kleenex appeared in front of her. She took it and dabbed a little more.

"Darn that brother of ours, he always manages to remind me that he really is a good guy now and then. He grew up after all."

"Yes, he did. And he knows that was a lot of your doing." The voice wasn't female. She whirled around to find Cade standing there. The look in his eyes made her want to tear up even more. "You raised him to be the man and father he is today. Everyone in that room knows it. You are greatly loved, Victoria Parker. I just don't think you realize how much sometimes. You have affected people that you probably don't even realize along the way because that is the woman you are."

Music began to play loudly. Tori stopped what she was about to say and pocketed the Kleenex. "That is awfully loud and sounds…"

"That would be the second part of my gift. We better get in there." He took her hand, and she didn't have time to react as they entered the dining room to find a full group of mariachis serenading the birthday girl who looked to be in absolute heaven.

"You brought mariachis?" She whispered her amazement beside the man.

"Matt mentioned he needed to find a record to play at her party. And I happen to know the leader of the group. They play once a month for the cattlemen's dinners. He was happy to bring them to serenade Jillie with a couple of songs. Hope you don't mind?"

She shook her head. She didn't trust her voice. At that point they broke into 'Happy Birthday' and it was amazing. She looked at Jillie and remembered how sad she had been on their shopping day about not having a mother of her own. But she would always know how very much she was surrounded by love, and she had to admit that the man standing behind her made a lot of her special day just that. If he had ulterior motives, she would deal with that later. She could be grateful in the moment. A gentle pressure on his hand from hers and he looked down at her. She mouthed the words 'thank you' and he gave her one of those warm smiles that always seemed to go straight to her heart. She turned back to the party.

☆

THAT WARM FEELING they had shared didn't last long. Once the party was over and Jillie had retired to the living room to watch one of the videos that Cassie had bought her, the grown-ups gathered in the kitchen to put away the last remnants of the party. She loaded the dishwasher; Cassie cleared the tables and Matt had trash duty. Cade took care of the tall stuff…taking down the decorations and then putting away items that needed to go in high cabinets. He would not think of leaving when the others tried to shoo him away.

"I'm sorry that I won't be here for Saturday's party," Cassie said as she put the lid on a pan of leftovers. "But duty calls and I must go."

"Funny how the call of duty coincides with the party that was to be outside now being moved in here—and twenty screaming girls and boys running amok is something that you are going to hate to have to miss indeed." Tori spoke with a tongue-in-cheek overtone.

"Well, I have news for both of you," Matt said. "You don't have to worry about rain and having all of them inside with little to do. Our friend Cade has offered a solution, which I gladly accepted."

Silence fell for a variety of reasons. Most of them seemed centered on the woman standing at the sink, her eyes zeroed on her brother. "Explain."

Matt realized his mistake too late. He should have waited with his news. Luckily, it seemed that Cade was ready to throw himself on the sword.

"It does look like rain most of the day—in fact, even the

night before—so everything will be wet and muddy no matter when the rain comes on Saturday. I have a large show arena that is covered and heated. It has a clean cement flooring in half of it. I have the manpower to transform it to whatever Jillie might want. And if we get the word out to your invited guests tomorrow, then all will know what to expect and where to come. Jillie just needs to tell me if she would like it."

"Wow, that is amazing," Cassie began but then became quiet.

"I see. That would certainly be a problem-solver. What does Jillie want?" asked Tori.

Matt stepped to the doorway and called for Jillie to join them. She was there in no time.

"We have a question for you." Tori stepped in and took over. "In case of rain on Saturday we have two options for you to decide which you would prefer. The first option is that we have the party here in my house like we have done before when it was bad weather. We still were able to decorate and have games and all the food." She took a breath before continuing, "The second option is that the party would be moved to Mr. Lockwood's barn and your friends could go to the party there inside where it's dry also. It's your decision."

Jillie did not hesitate. "A barn? How awesome! No one has done that before. And could there be animals around? Real ones? Not stuffed ones? And that means we could run a lot better and make noise and no one would really care. That would be so fun."

Tori knew she was defeated. *Keep smiling.*

"Well, it appears that live animals beat out stuffed ones in my house. I hope you know what you've just let yourself in for?" And she shot a pointed look in Cade's direction.

He nodded. "Oh, I think I understand quite well. And I look forward to hosting all of you and Jillie's friends this coming weekend."

"Matt will be happy to help of course. Won't you?" She next fixed her glare on him.

"Right…anything that is needed. We don't want to be an imposition."

"I never offer anything that I don't want to…and it is, after all, about Jillie's day. And with that decision made, I better get moving and make certain all will be ready for a barn birthday."

"Thanks again, for my great surprises." Jillie offered one last hug. Which he returned with a huge smile on his face.

"You are most welcome. See you Saturday." He didn't venture a look at his hostess as she had already turned back to her cleaning.

Jillie went back to her television. Cassie made an excuse to start packing. Matt was left. He moved to stand against the counter close to his sister.

"It makes sense, Tori. And it was a great offer. Jillie is over the moon."

"As she should be," Tori said, scrubbing a particularly tough bit of dried food on a pan in the sink.

"It's because of the rain threat that he offered. I should have told you after we were alone. If we had sunshine and blue skies it would be held right here as always. It isn't a slight in any way. Please don't take it personally."

Tori gave up on the scrubbing. She looked at her brother. "I'm glad that Jillie is going to have an awesome party. Her friends will all come…plus some…because who wouldn't like to be invited to a party of any kind on the famous Lockwood Ranch? It will be fine. I will be fine. Now go get your little girl home to bed. There's still school tomorrow."

"Yes, ma'am." He grinned, back to his old self. They shared a hug, and he was gone to collect his child and give Cassie a goodbye hug. Tori attacked the pan once again with a renewed vengeance.

Thankfully, Cassie made no mention of what had transpired, probably figuring she had said enough already on the subject. They hugged at the garage, and she left, back to her assignment, which always remained not for disclosure. Between her brother, a sheriff, and her sister, a DEA agent, and her other brother, a U.S. Marshal, she had more than enough experience in keeping secrets and not asking questions.

Later that week she dressed for her day and needed to bring in her new cushion from the front porch rocker just in case the rain began before she returned home. Opening the door, she almost stepped on something lying outside the doorway. She bent down and retrieved it.

It was one stem…a huge pink gerbera daisy…one stem only with a pink ribbon tied around its middle and a card attached to it. She read the message. *'Forgive me? C.'*

Well, at least he hadn't filled her porch with flowers. Just one this time, and it probably meant more than all the others from the office bouquet. He was trying to apologize. He was trying to do better as he promised. And this way, no one would know she had even received anything. It was just between the two of them. Cade Lockwood was a huge problem. Her life had been so simple until she had to push him into listening to her about those blasted springs. Now, she had no idea what to do. But she was afraid a good dose of heartbreak was headed her way. It was something she had guarded against in her life. She had trusted once before, believed in the possibility of a fairy tale. But she had been younger, and it became a learning experience. To keep her focus on what mattered the most: her family. And she had, until she met up with a tough cowboy one day who would shake up her world.

She had worried about running into Cade at some point in town and what she would say to him. But it hadn't happened. He hadn't come by the office. He hadn't left any messages. Three days of silence. Was she supposed to seek him out? He did put a question mark on the card. Meaning he expected her response? Well, it could wait for the party, which was the next day.

The thunder began to roll at midnight. Lightning woke her up at one in the morning and there was little sleep after that. The morning dawned overcast and rain still threatened in the distance. She had heard from Matt that they were at the ranch, and she would not believe what all Cade and his men had done for Jillie. It was up to her to arrive at the ranch gates at a precise time. She would arrive fifteen minutes after the party would begin. Sounded like another big entrance to Tori. The limo was getting a workout.

Jillie had decreed that the outfits of the day were to be

ranch/cowboy wear. And that was why Tori had taken her shopping to the ranching store in town and come out with Jillie outfitted from head to toe in jeans, fringed vest, western shirt, cowgirl hat and a pair of pink boots with rhinestones on the toes. Tori shook her head. And they weren't leaving the store before Jillie had made certain her aunt looked the part. Which basically entailed a new blue western shirt to go with the jeans she had several of in the closet already. And then she bought her first pair of boots…brown ones with no rhinestones. And a brown cowgirl hat that looked surprisingly good on her as decreed by Jillie. She added her own leather vest she often kept in the closet for rodeos and things along those lines when she had to attend as mayor. She was surprised when no limo appeared at the house. She and Jillie set off to Lockwood Ranch in her vehicle. As they approached, there was a difference from her last visit.

Cowboys were showing people where they could park on a freshly laid gravel parking area just inside the gates. When she and Jillie stepped out of the car, a familiar face greeted them. It was Nate, the foreman who had come with a crew that day to fix her gutters. He gave a big smile to them both and a special welcome to the birthday girl. "Are we going to ride on that wagon like others are doing?" Jillie asked with excitement.

"Nope…we are going to let them get ahead of you all. Then we have a special ride for you. Stand right here and don't turn around…either of you…until I tell you to do so, okay?"

Jillie bobbed her head in excitement. Tori nodded. There was a sound of wagon wheels behind them and horses stomping their feet.

"Okay, ladies, meet your ride."

They turned and Tori stood in silence taking it in while Jillie was faster to react. "Oh my, Aunt Tori…look…it's like on television in the westerns. Are we really going to ride in that?"

Nate nodded. "Yes, sirree, you bet. We don't bring this special stagecoach out for just anyone. That's why we added the ballons to the back. It's special just for you. Let's hop aboard." He opened the door and picked up Jillie and stood her inside. He offered his hand to Tori as she maneuvered the small step and the carriage of the wagon moved a bit as she stepped inside and took a seat beside her niece. Nate closed the door. "Sorry about those springs in there, ladies. They're original and not easy to take but you don't have far to go. Have fun!"

Jillie was glued to the open window, taking all in as the team of four horses turned them to head up the drive about a half-mile distant from where the house would be. But Tori noticed that they were heading off to the left on a smaller road she hadn't seen before. They were going past where the house was and continued over a little rise and there below was a huge, cavernous barn structure where there was clearly a party waiting. Balloons galore around the double doors that stood open and music from a live country trio was playing and could be heard outside. Dozens of Jillie's classmates and even teachers and some parents were waiting, the children clapping and cheering. Tori had to fight back the moisture that threatened as the magnitude of happiness coming from her niece's eyes was so worth it. These would be memories to replace those sad ones when they came along.

Matt waited for the horses to pull the coach up to the sidewalk. Then he opened the door and Jillie fairly jumped into his arms. He moved away to set her on drier ground, and she was engulfed by her friends.

Tori came out more slowly and was glad when a hand appeared from the tall cowboy who had swung down from the seat above to assist her. She looked up and almost did take a nosedive off the step until the man caught her and steadied her descent. Once on solid footing, she took a good look. Cade had been their driver all along and neither of them had noted it, they were so enthralled with the coach's arrival. He was dressed for the part more so than normal. Leather chaps with fringe and the Lockwood brand down their length, which obviously might have been one of his rodeo staples. Spurs jangled as he moved, and a bright blue bandana was around his neck. He could have been right out of a Remington painting.

"This is far above what was expected. You know that right?"

"Well, ma'am—" even he had his best John Wayne drawl going; it wasn't half bad "—we cowboys don't do things just halfway. We do aim to please our ladies."

Our ladies wasn't lost on Tori. It sent her pulse rate to high alert.

"And the answer is yes." She turned and joined Matt and the others as they moved inside the building. There was his answer. She had decided to forgive him. She didn't look back but concentrated on all the surprises to come.

Cowboys got into the fun along the way, bringing in

some live animals for petting. And some of the ranch's kids also joined in and Jillie took to them right away. There were long tables of finger foods: burgers, sandwiches, cookies, chips, popcorn machines, lemonade, and she just couldn't believe what all was there for the partygoers to enjoy whether they felt hungry or not. As she stood with some of the parents watching the children enjoying it all, she felt Matt grab her hand and pull her over to where the crowd was filling up the stands in front of some chutes.

"You have to see this," he said. Chute one opened and out raced like the wind a lamb…more like a teenaged-size lamb with a child on its back. He lasted three seconds before he hit the plowed dirt. He jumped up and ran back to do it again. Three more emptied the chutes and one little boy made it to the eight-second mark.

She saw Cade's tall form and Matt left her to join him behind the chutes. The next chute was set to go and it looked like Cade was going to stand out front and pull the gate. Matt was doing chute duty. The gate flew open and the lamb shot off. And she stood in disbelief. Jillie was under the pink helmet and protective jacket, and she was yelling up a storm but in a good way and hanging on for dear life. She made it to six seconds and then landed in the dirt. Cade was there to help her get her footing. She turned and waved to the crowd. Then came running to Tori who had made it to the edge of the arena. "Did you see, Aunt Tori? Wasn't that the best thing ever? I want to go do it again. Keep watching. She headed back to where Matt stood waiting, grinning from ear to ear.

"I ran out of flowers, but Jillie told me you love cotton

candy." Cade approached and held out a fluffy pink one to her. "I figured I might need to apologize again when you saw her come out of the chute."

She took the candy he offered. "This seems to be a habit of yours. But just so you know, for the next apology, I also love popcorn with lots of butter." She turned and walked toward a group of Jillie's friends' parents. Let him think on that one for a while.

Jillie was in her element the rest of the afternoon. In fact, she even had her first dance with one of the ranch kids who shyly walked up and asked if she wanted to learn to line dance with the rest of them. She was game. She and Matt stood watching from the sideline. She couldn't swear but she thought she noted a time or two where he turned his head away and might have wiped something from his eye. She smiled. She had done the same thing. Their little Jillie was growing up.

"You're breaking the rules of the ranch today." Cade had moved to sit on the bench beside her. It was a quiet spot since most of the action had moved down a bit into the center of the arena.

"I did? What? I'm sorry but..."

"I'm teasing. It's just that no one can look as sad as you just did on a great day like today. So, I asked myself what can I do to get that smile back? And the answer came to me. Come on...come with me." He was practically pulling her up from her seat. She went along in order to not draw attention to them. He led her out one door and into a long barn with stalls on each side.

"Where are we going?"

"To see an old friend of yours." He kept walking. He finally stopped midway, and she saw what he was talking about. She leaned her hands on the open stall door bottom.

"Ladybug! Hello, sweet one. Do you remember me?" The horse obviously did as she moved to stand with her head over the gate, her eyes soft and big as she blew out a soft breath in hello.

Tori remembered she loved to have her nose rubbed and she did just that. The animal nudged her to continue.

"Now you'll have to stand here all afternoon and do nothing else," Cade said watching the pair.

"That wouldn't bother me a bit. You don't know how lucky you are to be able to do this anytime you want."

"Well, we do have other things to keep us busy on the ranch besides rubbing a horse's nose. But if you would like to volunteer for the job, feel free to apply. The owner might just sign you up."

"You think so?" She grinned in response to his.

"But whatever would Destiny's River do without their mayor?"

"Haven't you heard of multitasking? I am very good at it. I can do both."

"Then you're hired."

"Seriously, this is what I pictured growing up before things got crazy and all. I thought about being a vet even. Silly dreams of a kid."

"Not so silly. And you can come out here and visit Ladybug anytime. And if this cranky old rancher might be around, well he might be willing to take you two out riding."

She looked at him with silent regard for a couple moments. "It isn't nice to try to bribe a government official with a horse."

He laughed and shook his head. "Well, I mean it. You give your name at the gate—you are already on the list—and you can come out here anytime and visit Ladybug. The hands all know this horse belongs to the mayor. So whenever the job gets too much or people make you mad—present company included—let this be your quiet spot away from it all. No strings attached, Tori. You deserve it."

"Why are you doing this? What is the game?" She might as well lay it on the line.

"What do you mean?"

"Look, we couldn't stand each other in the beginning. Then we took a business trip. And you actually paid attention and now we're going to see a lot of people get really good help. That should have been that. But now my whole family is involved with you. We're having dinners and…" She was fumbling it.

"And I kissed you. That's what changed. It's no longer professional. It's personal. And it is uncharted territory for me. I was never going to let anything, or anyone get too personal. But then an irritating woman came along who didn't care what my last name was or how many fans I might have. She didn't have any problem putting me in my place."

"I'm a novelty to you," Tori said. "Because I'm different. I'm not all sleek and sophisticated like the women in your usual life. That's more your speed. And I won't play games. I'm not made for that. One man one woman…no space for a third or fourth party…or more. And it isn't fair trying to bribe me with over-the-top things for my niece or knowing what a horse does to me and telling me it's all mine. It isn't and it never will be. So, please just let it go."

She walked away. It was the hardest thing she ever did but it had to be done. Make the cut quick…that is what she'd learned from the days of being tossed around as a child. Somehow, she'd get past all of this and things would be normal again. Maybe not tomorrow or the next day…even the days after that. But it would come. Just no looking back.

Chapter Sixteen

TWO WEEKS. TWO weeks was how long it had been since her speech in the barn at Lockwood Ranch. She should feel good about the fact that she had neither seen nor heard from Cade in all that time. Matt and even Maggie seemed to steer clear of mentioning him around her. If they did, in Maggie's case, it was that things were progressing with the springs and the medical communities were all on board. Cade Lockwood was doing everything he had promised.

And she should be glad of that. It would mean so much to so many—help so many. Sitting on her front porch with her morning coffee, she had garnered another homeless cat who had wandered up and never left. That was fine. The weather was turning and Easter and then spring would come out in full force. She'd have to get Jillie's basket of goodies planned out. Plan the family dinner. Do all the usual things. Three out of four cabins were rented and two of them were long term. She liked having the small cabins, each decorated in their own style, instead of strangers coming and going in the house as Addie had done with the previous boarding house.

Primrose Inn would have an incredible garden bursting with color in the spring. That's as it should be. One of the tenants turned out to have a green thumb and had already made some inroads in preparation for the spring.

Her thoughts in the early morning sunrise and the evening sunset often went to Ladybug…hoping someone was giving her the nose rubs she enjoyed. And as much as she hated to admit it, Cade would often intrude in those moments too. She thought by cutting him out of her life for good that it would all ease up. But it only brought the realization that he had stolen into her heart, and it would take a lot longer to rid herself of his memory. She was used to heartbreak in her life, but this was so different and so much more painful, which only seemed to increase in intensity rather than decrease. She would keep moving forward just as she always did. That was her plan.

The phone rang. So much for the peace and quiet. She opened the cell and saw a familiar name. She was already smiling. "Who is this stranger calling me?"

"Okay, I deserved that. But I don't have long to talk. I'm about to get a case and I am passing through your neck of the woods. How about lunch?"

"Well, let me check my social calendar." She paused. "Okay I can fit you in."

"I'll meet you at Tillie's at eleven thirty. Bye."

"Bye to you, too." But he was already gone. The smile had remained on her face. It's just what the doctor ordered. So she needed to get a move on. Get to the office and then to her lunch date. She grinned for the first time in a long time.

Tillie's was crowded but she had called ahead and explained the circumstance and Tillie had come through for her. She took her right to a table in the corner of the big room, next to the window. It was nice and she could see most of the goings on around the square. She was on the lookout for a familiar face. She didn't hear anyone approaching.

"Looking for me by any chance?"

She jumped up and hugged the man. The huge smile on her face summed it up. He was a welcome sight for sore eyes. He hugged her right back. Then he took off his hat and sat it on the corner of the table as they both sat down.

Tori couldn't stop smiling. "You look good. Tired maybe…a little older. But good. Now tell me how you really are."

"Still the mother hen, I see," he said. "I'm good. I've just been working a couple of cases that have kept me busy…lots of travel. But I have another assignment that will take me to the border for a while so this would be my only chance to see you. I would like to have seen Matt, but I hear he's tied up in the next county on a court case. I'll catch him next time."

"We missed you at Jillie's party, but she understood. She did love your gift."

"She's growing like a weed from the last photo Matt sent."

Tillie came up at that moment and they both knew what they wanted, and she gave him a quick hug and she was off to turn in the orders.

"Nothing changes around here…still the best place to eat in town by the looks of the crowd. And now it's time you tell me what you've been up to, Mayor Parker. And don't leave anything out."

She gave him the highlights of her time in office with

one or two minor adjustments. The burgers arrived and he took a quick bite. "Okay so now give me the scoop on this Lockwood character that Cassie has told me so much about. When do I meet him and how much would you miss him if he disappeared?"

"That's not amusing, Rance." She gave him a level look. "And not what a U.S. Marshal should be saying in public."

"And you're stalling. Is it serious?"

"No. It's done. So, you can stand down, Mr. Lawman. And remember, your sister can take care of herself."

He reached over and tugged on her ponytail like he used to do to irritate her as a kid. "Just making sure that my sister knows I'm just a phone call away. And I do have a lot of friends I can call too."

"You and your brother and your sister can rest assured that I'm just fine. Now finish your burger and I'll walk you to your truck."

Ten minutes later they were standing by his vehicle, which he had parked in the Reserved for Official Vehicles area. "I already miss you. Please don't let it be so long before I see you again. We all miss your stubborn hide…now and then."

He reached up and brushed her cheek. "Hey knock it off. Since when have you become so weepy? I'll be back, I promise. Until then, I'm just a phone call away. Take care, sis." He gathered her into a tight bear hug. Then he was in his truck and flashing a hand in a wave as he drove away.

No use standing around moping when there was work to do inside. She squared her shoulders and headed into the courthouse.

☆

"WHERE HAVE YOU been? You drifted off in some kind of trance?" David Prescott was one of the men at the table where Cade was sitting and having a business lunch of sorts. But his mind went blank when he had seen Tori walk in and take a seat at a table for two across the room. He had just about made up his mind to walk over there when a tall cowboy walked in and headed straight for her. When she saw him, she had lit up like a Christmas tree and practically jumped into his arms. Cade knew he had not seen the cowboy around before and he wanted to know what was going on.

He tried not to stare but it was clear they were more than friends and she looked at him like she couldn't get enough of him. The man's back was to him, but he did see him reach out and stroke her hair and she seemed not to mind that at all. Then they left together, and he made an excuse to take the bill for the table and go to the front to pay for both of them. He could see outside better that way. But he didn't care for the fact that she looked so sad to see him leave—but not before they shared an embrace that set his blood pressure rising. Who was this guy?

And then he noted something interesting. The guy had parked his truck in the reserved section like he had every right to be there. And she didn't seem the least bit concerned about that. In fact, he bet he wouldn't get towed. He left a generous tip because he wasn't paying attention and didn't respond when Tillie tried to tell him that. The rest of the afternoon was not good for the people who crossed his path.

So she had someone she was interested in? It didn't seem like someone she'd just met. Perhaps someone she was seeing when he met her? Or was this something that only occurred when the guy was passing through? Nothing made sense and it only irritated him not knowing. Well, if she had moved on just fine, then so be it. Lesson learned.

★

"I AM SO glad we were able to finalize the plans for the opening of the thermal springs, Cade," Maggie said as they came out of the council chambers. "I'm just sorry that our mayor couldn't have joined us. But she had a conference she had to speak at in Austin. She knows we'll handle things just fine and fill her in when she returns. I'll let you know when the last of the estimates have cleared."

"Thank you, Maggie." Cade turned and headed down the stairs. He gave a brief glance in the direction of the mayor's office door, but it was closed and he had no reason to have any business there anyway.

He had just about made it to the front glass doors when Matt saw him and stepped into the hall. "Hey, Cade, where you been keeping yourself?"

He shook hands with the sheriff. "I've been busy with the spring calving and bringing another pasture online…clearing the mesquite and such."

"It is getting to be that time of year." Matt nodded. "Jillie asked about you. You are on her list of favorite people you know."

"That's an honor as far as I'm concerned. You need to

bring her out to ride soon."

"She'll love that. She's in a bit of tizz right now as she missed seeing Rance when he stopped by to see Tori a couple days ago."

Rance. Where had he heard that name before? Matt must have read his moment of confusion.

"Rance as in Ransom…our prodigal brother you have yet to meet."

"Your brother. That's right. Well, I am sorry that I didn't get to meet the remaining Parker. I suppose he'll be back soon?"

"I doubt it. He's got an assignment down in the valley. Of course, Tori is hoping he'll make it for Easter, as she is always hopeful where her errant siblings are concerned. We all went to Austin to have dinner with him last Easter. We'll see if he makes it. I'll make certain you get to meet him next time. I have a photo of him that I took on my phone of all of us. Let's see if I can bring it up."

"Have I ever seen him?"

"Here it is. He was giving us a tour of his office in the capital." He handed over the phone and the lights went off in Cade's brain. "He works in Austin."

"He's a U.S. Marshal. His office right now is temporarily in the capital building until their offices are ready over in the federal court building."

"I see. And he drives a vehicle that can park in any reserved space for law enforcement I imagine."

Matt looked at him for a moment. "That's correct."

"I do recall seeing him in that area a while back. I didn't know he was law enforcement at the time."

"I see. Well, too bad you two didn't get to meet. Maybe next time."

"Maybe. I'll look forward to it. Good to see you, Matt. Give Jillie a hello for me." Cade went on his way and his brain was spinning. *What an idiot.* All the time he had wasted being jealous over her brother. He needed to come up with a plan and the sooner the better.

☆

"MAGGIE, I AM really not that hungry. But if you insist I sit here and drink tea while you have something, be my guest."

"Thank you for joining me. And I know you would love these new recipes that Tillie is trying out. I'll get two just in case you change your mind."

"Well fancy seeing you here, Cade," Maggie said with a wide grin. "Do join us. We can go over some of the plans for the opening day now that you both are here."

Tori felt sure he would make an excuse to not stay but he smiled and took a seat.

"Hello, Tori, it's good to see you again. You're looking well."

They would have to make small talk.

"I'm fine, thank you. And you?"

"Could not be better. That does look delicious, Maggie."

"You should try it. Tillie is just amazing."

Tillie arrived with the rest of the plates of food and Maggie had just cut into her chicken breast when her phone rang. "Hello?" She listened for a moment or two. "Very well if it can't wait."

Maggie looked at them both and shook her head. "I am so sorry but I need to run over to Judge Spicer's courtroom right quick. I should be back shortly. I know you two will enjoy the food and don't let it get cold. I'll be right back." She didn't give either time to reply before she was halfway across the room.

"Well, I suppose we shouldn't let all this waste. How about some of these fresh rolls? I believe you once said they were favorites of yours." He passed the breadbasket over to her.

She was trying to figure out a good exit but then Maggie said she would be right back. Tori didn't like being put in such a spot.

"I understand you got to have a visit with your brother Rance?"

"I suppose Matt told you that?"

"Yes, he did mention it. I know that made you happy."

Silence.

"This is awkward," Cade finally said.

"Very much so."

"I've missed you."

Tori felt that pain in her chest at his words and knew her heart could be a traitor. "What am I supposed to say to that? I thought we weren't going to get personal if and when we saw each other around town?"

"Well, that hasn't worked real well for me. In fact, I admit I almost had your brother's truck towed from that reserved for lawmen space at the courthouse when he was here."

"What in the world? Why would you do such a thing?"

"I didn't know the person you were having such a great lunch with that day was in fact your brother. When I saw he was parked there, well I felt he might need to be towed… That's what you would have done, right? Thinking someone who couldn't read a sign had parked there anyway?"

"Have you lost your mind?"

"Possibly. And believe me, it hasn't been pleasant. And I noticed when I owned up to saying I missed you that you didn't respond. Guess that lets me know how much you did not miss my charming personality."

"Have you hit your head recently? You haven't spoken to me in almost a month now and here you are telling me how much you missed me? And expecting me to do the same to you?"

"If you recall, Tori, it wasn't I who walked away at Jillie's party. It was you. And I was trying to respect your wishes and give you space."

"Thank you for that. Too bad it couldn't have continued today."

"You know you should ask yourself why in the world that a grown man like me with a reasonably intelligent brain would want to subject himself to your sharp tongue and more rejection."

"I have no idea why."

"Think about it, Tori. Stop being mad and on your high horse long enough to consider that question. You aren't easy, Tori. But I'm still here. Give my regrets to Maggie. I'm sure we'll be seeing each other again." He stood up and left her sitting there with a table full of food and no one to eat it. She didn't know whether to throw something or scream. How dare he make it out to be her fault? And talk about her sharp tongue? Who rejected who? And she was running out of steam trying to stay angry. She was hurt. And she missed him. And he still looked too damn good and made her remember so many things she wanted to forget. She thought she was on her way to doing just that and then he had to come along and burst that bubble.

He missed her. Those words wouldn't go away. They were on an endless loop in her brain. They needed to stop. He was miserable? And he had seen her having lunch with an unknown male and it had made him mad? *Jealous.* And that thought gave her pause. It was good that he could know how it felt. She had felt that before him…in much the same way as she watched him and that woman that day. Who had turned out to be his half-sister. It wasn't pleasant he had said. That would be putting it mildly. Seeing him today and talking to him…it all came flooding back again and she felt miserable. They both had been hurting. But if he felt anything for anyone else…surely he wouldn't be that miserable?

She should have held her temper. They should have had a sensible discussion. But they couldn't. Because it was their hearts talking and not their brains. He said they would see each other again. Was that a warning? Or a promise? Why did she have a hope that it was the latter?

Tillie came over with a stack of to-go boxes. "Maggie said to give you these as she couldn't make it back. So you just heat it all up and enjoy later."

She smiled her thanks. And why did that surprise her? Maggie wasn't coming back. She was beginning to think she might have been set up. Interesting scenario. Well, she would be prepared next time.

Chapter Seventeen

THE NEXT TIME turned out to be the day that the springs were to be officially opened with a ribbon-cutting and a plaque-laying ceremony. It had been almost three weeks since the disaster at the café. Today there would be no ignoring. She would have to talk to him, pose for photos with him and generally make nice with him. She arrived with Maggie. And Matt was there and so was Jillie. Jillie had informed her that Cade had personally invited them. Well, she was glad. That meant she would have some supporters there and safety nets. The sooner it was all done the better.

"It's perfect weather today. Bright cloudless blue sky as only can be so glorious in Texas," Maggie proclaimed. "We are going to have your opening remarks, welcome et cetera. Then you will introduce me and I will introduce the hospital board and of course the Lockwood Foundation and Cade. Then you and he will step to the ribbon take the scissors…sort of like cutting a wedding cake." She laughed but neither Tori nor Cade did so. He had been on his best behavior welcoming guests to his ranch home, seeing that they had drinks and were made comfortable.

She had chosen to wear one of her 'power' suits as Cassie had called it. Her brilliant blue blazer with black turtleneck sweater and black slacks. She had swept her hair back into a

French braid. Cade was in a black western-cut suit looking every inch the wealthy rancher benefactor.

She was looking over her remarks once again in a quiet corner of the library. Cade found her there and shut the door behind him.

"You aren't nervous are you?" he asked by way of a conversation starter. "No need to be. You've got this. All the people really care about is being able to see the springs and eat the dinner we're providing. And all you really need to do is just smile and look beautiful, which you already do."

"I like to be prepared. You can wing it all you like."

"Well, after it is all said and done today, we need to find a moment to talk. And I already checked with Wallace. Your schedule is open the rest of the day."

"It's time," she said. "We don't want to keep people waiting."

He held the door open for her.

There was quite a crowd that had gathered for the ribbon cutting. And the press was there to record it all. Maggie nodded and Tori began the ceremony with a welcome to all and then a brief history of how the project came to be…a concerted effort by a small group of people wanting to help those who could benefit from the thermal pools in their therapy. Then she introduced Maggie who took it from there. When Cade went before the microphones he began very simply. "We are here today because of the vision of one person whose tenacious spirit and unflagging energy managed to prevail when others failed, one person who never gave up. We all owe a great deal of thanks to Mayor Victoria Parker for bringing us all here today." The applause was spontaneous and totally unexpected. She had no idea Cade was going to say such a thing. Moisture threatened and thankfully Maggie went on with introductions and gave her time to compose herself.

"Now, it's time to ask Mr. Lockwood and Mayor Parker to cut the ribbon to open the springs officially." Tori and Cade moved forward, the scissors were handed over and they both grasped the handles of the oversized implement. He looked at her and she at him and it would turn out to be a photo to embody that day. "This is because of you, Tori," he whispered. "Thanks for making me change my mind." Then they cut the ribbon and it fluttered to the ground to more applause.

People lined up to have a tour up to where the pools were ready to receive patients. Tori stepped back. She preferred to see the changes to the place after others had seen and left the area. She found Matt and Jillie and they moved to the large tent that had been set up with tables and food. She really couldn't eat very much as people kept stopping by their table to shake her hand and congratulate her on the hard work.

In a lull, she managed a sip of tea. Matt leaned closer and whispered some words. "You realize that the talk is that you are already to be elected mayor next summer again. The people like your style of getting things done, sis. Way to go."

That should have made her happy to know but it was hard to summon such a feeling. She was dreading what Cade wanted to talk about. As though her thoughts conjured him, he appeared moving in her direction. But he wasn't alone. The woman she had seen with him at the café, the one who parted from him with an embrace—the one he said was his family member—was walking straight for her. She stood. She thought better on her feet. Suddenly, she wished Matt and Jillie and Maggie and the others weren't at the table. But it was too late. Cade and the woman stopped beside her.

It wasn't Cade who spoke first.

"I've been wanting to meet you, Mayor Parker. I am a big fan of yours. I'm Selena Lockwood."

"How do you do?" Was that her pathetic-sounding voice? Tori wanted the floor to open and suck her to the other side of the world.

"Selena is indeed a fan of yours, Tori. She is also part of our legal team for the Lockwood Foundation. She lives not far from Austin, which is why most of you have never met her. But I felt she needed to be here today. And to meet Tori." Cade's gaze never left Tori's. "And if you would all keep her company, Tori and I have a meeting. We will rejoin you afterwards."

Cade's hand on her back guided her through the guests and then outside where she was able to take in some fresh air at last. His hand fell to her hand, and she didn't have the energy to disagree.

"Where are we going?"

"You need to see the changes we made. You haven't approved them."

"It's a little late for that isn't it?"

"If you don't approve, we will change it. That simple."

The climb was a little steep when done in high heels. But where there had been rocks before, there was a smooth cement walkway, complete with handrails and no steps.

Benches sat under the tall trees, now bare of leaves. A small building of native stone housed the restrooms and the dressing areas for males and females. They were all ADA compliant. And they were warm in the fall months and had AC in the warm weather. Another work area had room for therapy equipment that the onsite therapist could put to use.

"Now for the pools," he said and they stepped outside again. There were three pools that had been developed, which meant they had easy access for those who could walk into the pool and those who could not. There were emergency equipment boxes at each pool and phone service that went straight to the paramedics had been installed.

"It is still a work in progress. Patients will be referred to a therapist who will schedule time for them in one of these pools. Weekends will be closed to allow the springs to settle. Does it meet with your approval? Say the word and if we need to add something we will."

"You managed to do all of this in less than three months."

"When you have work crews already that is half the battle. But this is all because of you. You fought for it. You had to put up with me and my arrogance because some crazy woman dared to challenge me on my own land. But also, I remembered a few things that my grandfather taught me. And I know that this is something he would be very proud to know has happened here. There are still springs that are untouched. He would have been proud that the Lockwood name would be associated with something that can do good for so many others. And you were the catalyst. Thank you, Tori, for not backing down."

"It is perfect, Cade. Thank you for doing this."

"Well, now we have all the thanks out of the way, we need to clear some air. And this is a pretty good place to do it. Grandfather would approve of this, too."

"I'm listening."

"Good, let me finish and then you can talk. You best sit down."

Tori moved to a nearby bench and did just that, her hands folded in her lap, trying to stay calm because she had no idea what was coming next.

"I'm stubborn. And remember you promised not to speak until I'm done. But I have reasons why I'm not very trustful of women—from past experiences. But then I met a woman who did not care how many buckles there were or what bank account I had. You just expected me to listen and do the right thing. You were scary. And I hadn't a clue how to figure you out. So it took some time. I had to listen. I watched. And I had to admit that you might be the real deal.

"And then I realized that getting to know you wasn't that easy. You had your own walls. You might not like what I say next. But here goes. You are amazing. But you don't see that. Your family has you on a pedestal because you have been parent and sibling and so much more for so long. You put every person ahead of you. And you expect nothing in return. You aren't used to others wanting to help you. So you pull away. You aren't used to others getting too close. Because you don't trust that they won't leave or disappoint you. They might break your heart...because that is depending on others and giving them some control.

"I didn't figure that out right away, so I made some mistakes. I should have told you right away about Selena, but I didn't, and that was wrong. But I've realized that my grandfather was a wise man, yet he could also make mistakes, and it cost him his one true love in life. He taught me to walk in my own steps and not his. I had to remind myself of that. That's when I decided that there would be no more games, no more misinformation, no more wasting time. I know what I want now and for the rest of my life. The question is, what do you want? For *you*...not anyone else in your family. Take a leap of faith, Tori. I'll catch you. I promise you that I won't be going anywhere. But you have to decide. The floor is yours."

"I will own that a lot of what you say is true. I am not so much stubborn as determined. I did have to learn to fight to protect those I love from an early age. People lied. People disappointed along the way. So, I decided that I would trust me and me alone. I would do my best to give those I love—my family—all that they deserved. I worked for that. And I found Destiny's River. It spoke to something inside me that had been missing. I made it home. And I ran for mayor for much the same reason. There were things I knew needed to change in order to help people who lived here, and I believed that I could do it. And the community needed the springs for those who were ill and hurting.

"When you say I had—have—walls to keep those who aren't my family away, I have to own that too. For so long, I've had to be everything and if I failed, my family would be harmed. I have issues trusting someone else besides myself. So I got used to being the one to handle everything. That carried over not just in my family but also in my work and my relationships. I couldn't trust you when you came along and tried to break down the wall. Instead, I became more defensive. What could you possibly want with someone like me? Our worlds are far apart. And I pushed you away because it would keep the pain away. Silly as it sounds, that's the truth of it all. I'm not easy. I own that."

"You are definitely not easy," Cade admitted with a hint of a grin. "But that is part and parcel of how you have survived. I am amazed at the strength you have, day in and day out, to protect your family, to look out for them and love them. Then to take on issues in the town that others have and champion them with the same energy and tenacity. I think at some point, I realized how much I wanted to be included in that group. I was jealous in a weird sort of way. And I experienced this incredible desire to step in and help shoulder the burden. Maybe burden isn't the right word. But everyone needs someone to share the load with. I wanted to be the one to do that for you. But you just wouldn't have it. Seems the more I tried, the more determined you became.

"But then something my grandfather said more than once as I was growing up made sense to me at last. Anything truly worth having is worth fighting for with all you've got. I saw what happened when my grandfather finally gave up on his dream. I didn't want to be that person. So I didn't run away. I met you head-on.

"The truth is all I want between you and me. Good and bad. I want to share it all. I don't want to change you from the incredible woman you are. I want you to feel you can lay your head on my shoulder when things get to be too much. Rest and let me share the load. Then when you are ready, you can take on the world again, and I will cheer you on. And you will do the same for me. I think we both can work on doing that. And speaking of truth, I will begin with this.

"I love you, Tori Parker. Plain and simple. You're worth fighting for. Every day, good or bad, I'll be there for you. That's why I wasn't about to give up. Life with you would be the greatest adventure of them all. And the most amazing. The question is what is it that you want for *your* life?"

☆

CADE LOVES ME. He said it. And he means it. My heart and my brain finally agree.

Tori stood. Truth. Cards on the table. "What I want is to have someone love me for who I am. I don't want to be on a pedestal. I do want to know that there is another shoulder there in case I need it. That I won't be perfect or right all the time, but I can fail and the world won't end. I want to have someone care and be present. No lies, no misunderstandings...we can always talk."

"Is that all?"

"Well, there is one more thing."

Cade was listening intently.

"A horse. My own horse. And someone who likes to watch the sunrise and sunset and hold my hand through each and every one of them. The person who will be my home. And I will be his."

Cade shook his head. Had she gone too far?

"I do believe that a horse of your own is very much doable. And beginning my day and ending it with you sounds like one heck of a deal."

"What do you want?"

Her heart started somersaulting in her chest. He slowly sank to one knee.

"*You*, Victoria 'Tori' Parker. For all the days of my life and beyond. Will you marry me?" A diamond solitaire held between his fingers cast its brilliance in the waning sunlight.

This was the dream held tightly within her for so long. And this was the man who came in answer to her prayer. The dream she was always afraid to voice in case it would disappear and never come again. The wall came tumbling down.

"Yes, Cade Lockwood. I very much would like to marry you." The ring slipped onto her ring finger. Then she was lifted off her feet and the kiss was one to seal their promises. She was home and it wasn't a dream.

Epilogue

Two months later

THE GARDEN WAS bursting with color. Bright yellow daffodils, tulips in reds, pinks, yellows, white, hyacinths purple and pink. Baskets and urns held arrangements of brilliant yellow and pink glads with roses in pale to bright pink. Butterflies waited to be released. The gazebo with its intricate scrollwork and fresh white paint, stood in the center ready to welcome the bridal couple. White chairs sat in a semicircle around the gazebo. Two harpists sat in a corner of the wraparound porch playing softly as guests arrived.

Jillie sat in the window seat in the second-floor bedroom watching the goings-on below. Her dress was a soft pink confection with a full skirt of tulle that fell to her ankles. Her hair had been curled to fall down the center of her back. A headband with sparkles in pale pink sat on her head.

Cassie came into the room in her bridal outfit…also in a shade of pink darker than Jillie's. It was street-length with a full skirt also of tulle over satin. Her hair had been swept up on top of her head and held in place with a glittering clip.

"You need to get your shoes on your feet now, Jillie. We're going downstairs soon."

"But where is Tori? She said I could see her dress before we went down."

"You can but only with your shoes on. Get a move on or we'll have to leave you up here."

"I'm going to check on her and I'll call you when she's ready." She turned and remembered something. She took the basket with its pink petals out of the florist's box. "You need to keep up with this now. You remember what you're supposed to do when we get to the porch?"

"I know. I've been practicing."

Cassie smiled. She had watched her niece from a window yesterday when she thought no one was watching. She had done the walk over and over. She took her job as flower girl very seriously.

"I'll call you."

Cassie left her alone. She crossed over the hall to another bedroom and was about to go inside. A voice stopped her.

"When does this party get started?"

"It's about time." Cassie grinned and did a quick skip over to wrap her arms around the cowboy's neck.

"Hey," he said with a laugh. "Don't wrinkle this fancy suit. There might be some women in attendance that I want to impress."

Cassie stood back and made a show of straightening the lapels of the gray western-cut suit. "Excuse me," she said with mock contriteness. "I forgot how conceited my little brother could be. But I warn you that any women in attendance today will only have eyes for the groom. You've met your match. But maybe you can help patch up those broken hearts a bit."

"Ouch." He grimaced. "I came here to be insulted by my sibling? But who knows, maybe there will be one or two men here today that might be willing to take you on. Otherwise, you could possibly be the last old maid in our family since Tori is walking down that aisle today."

"You might remember that our sister also carries a gun, little brother. And she is a better shot than you are." Matt came up the last step of the staircase and met the handshake of his brother.

"Thanks for the reminder." Rance grinned. "I hear that you and I are walking the bride down the aisle today?"

"Change of plans," Matt said. "I'm taking my rightful place beside the groom. I've been elevated to best man. You'll have to steady the bride down the aisle. Think you can handle that?"

"As long as I'm not the one standing in the groom's spot in this wedding, I can do a great job."

"One of these days," Cassie said with a shake of her head, "you won't run fast enough and we'll be laughing at you as you say those vows."

"I flew in here to be subjected to your taunts? I don't think so. Where is this bride at?" Rance said. "Let's get this party started."

Cassie turned and motioned for them to follow. "Matt, please get Jillie and let her come in also."

When Matt had rejoined them with an excited daughter in tow, she became even more animated when she saw her uncle Rance. He swept her up and around in his arms. "Now here is the prettiest girl at this wedding. Are you going to dance with your old uncle today?"

She nodded quickly. "Every dance. And we have a lot of cake to eat, too."

Cassie opened the door and ushered them all inside.

They stopped and took in the sight, silence replacing the laughter.

Tori stood in front of the full-length mirror, the seamstress—having helped her with her gown—was now adjusting the full-length veil. Stunning white lace lay over a pale pink lining. The sleeveless, heart-shaped bodice had a wide swathe of pale pink around the waist and slender ribbons fell down the back to the edge of the skirt. When she walked, the skirt would flow around her softly. The veil was full and edged in the same lace all the way down to form a semi-train behind her. The dress was perfect. Tori had never been more beautiful. Cassie tucked another Kleenex into the edge of her demi-glove…to be on the safe side.

"Is it that bad that all of you are just staring and not saying anything?" Tori asked, looking at them in the mirror behind her.

"It's you. Perfect. Gorgeous." Callie found her voice first.

"You look like a real Cinderella," Jillie pronounced in awe.

"Not bad, sis," Rance said, something strange stuck in his throat.

"Perfect. Just perfect." Matt seemed to have something in one eye and turned his attention to straightening his daughter's dress. Then he stepped forward and stood in front of his sister. "I need to go and give some support to a nervous groom. But…well, you've got this. It will be the easiest walk you'll ever take. And the one you deserve more than anyone. Love you, sis." He bent and placed a quick kiss on her cheek. And then left the room.

"If you cry now, you'll ruin your makeup," Cassie said. "I'll cry enough for both of us."

"I hear that I have the honor of giving you away, today." Rance spoke up, moving to give her a hug. He stepped back and gave her one of his usual grins that he often teased her with. "I always wanted to do that when we were growing up as little kids. But now...well, it doesn't seem like a great idea for some reason."

Tori shook her head. "None of you can get rid of me that easily. I'll be here as usual. Full-time big sister. It's a tough job but someone has to do it."

☆

"SO IS THE bride ready? She's upstairs, right?"

Matt shook his head as he looked at the man in the silver-gray western tuxedo, adjusting his hat on his head for the tenth time in front of the mirror. "Rest easy. I just checked on her and she is here and still planning to meet you in the garden in a few minutes. We tried to talk her out of it, but she wouldn't be bribed even. No changing Tori's mind when she's determined. And she asked the same question about you. Wanted to make sure you had showed up."

Cade grinned and turned to face the man.

"You didn't tell her that I showed up two hours early, right? Don't want to appear too eager, you know."

Matt laughed. "I think that ship has already sailed. We're going to have to keep you from running down that aisle, I have a feeling."

"You just might," Cade agreed. Then his gaze sobered as

it met Matt's. "Look, I'm glad that you agreed to stand up with me today. It means a lot. I know we haven't had too much time to sit down and just talk lately, but I want you to know…all of you," he amended. "I will mean every word of the vows I take today. I intend to spend every day I have in this life making Tori happy. She deserves all of that and much more. And I feel very honored that you all have welcomed me into the fold. It means a lot more than I can say. You are my family now and that is something that I will try my best to be worthy of each day."

Matt walked closer and slowly put out his hand. Cade accepted it. "We all know that you love our sister. A blind man could see and feel that. And knowing how Tori feels about you…well, none of us could have asked for better in a life's partner for her than you. You are a good man and we know you will take good care of each other. Cherish each other and each day you have."

Cassie breezed in at that moment.

"The minister is here and the guests are being seated. Sun is bright, sky is blue, and there is a bride coming down the aisle in ten minutes. Take your places, gentlemen. And, Matt, you have the ring right?"

"That is at least the twentieth time you have asked me that question today, Cassie," Matt replied.

"Well?" She was waiting.

"It is right here," and he patted his jacket pocket.

"Very well. See you both at the altar." She gave a wink and was gone.

Cassie nodded to the harpists, and they began the music. Jillie began her walk across the porch and down the runner toward the gazebo. Flowers were tossed along the way with great skill. Cade grinned at her and winked as she approached. She winked back.

Cassie walked the aisle next, smiling at the guests as she went. Cade met her grin with one of his. Then the music changed, and the guests rose. The bride appeared, escorted by her brother Rance. The guests were not disappointed in watching the groom's reaction as he watched his bride walk toward him. His gaze never wavered from hers. He came down the two steps to meet her. Rance kissed her cheek and then gave her hand over to Cade.

The vows were spoken from their hearts. Tori's voice held a bit of trembling at first, but then there was a gentle, warm pressure on her hands that were encased in Cade's. His strength flowed into hers and his silent message was in his gaze. *We've got this.* And her heart took flight and so did any nerves.

Cade made his vows strong and sure. The prayers were beautiful blessings for long life and happiness. The preacher pronounced them husband and wife and as the couple kissed, hundreds of butterflies took flight throughout the garden.

The reception began, the cake was cut, guests partied. Cade thanked Jillie for their dance and went in search of his bride. He found her in the gazebo. Her face was aglow with the golden rays of sunset. He moved to slip his arms around her and she leaned against him.

"A perfect wedding. I'm glad you wanted to have the wedding here in your garden instead of the ranch. It turned out to be beautiful. What's on my wife's mind?"

Tori nodded, her gaze still on the sunset. "I came here a young girl with a stray cat and stayed because of the sunset. It was so beautiful that day when I stepped off the bus. I was scared. I had no idea what I was doing but I had to find a home. And that sunset spoke to my heart. I stayed and now here I am with another perfect sunset and my heart is so complete. I am not a stranger in this garden, and I'm not scared. I am home. Now and forever in Destiny's River. In your arms."

The End

More Books by Debra Holt

Texas Heritage series

Book 1: *The Texas Cowboy's Proposal*
Book 2: *The Texas Cowboy's Lady*
Book 3: *The Texas Cowboy's Rescue*
Book 4: *The Texas Cowboy's Christmas Miracle*

The Tremaynes of Texas series

Book 1: *Capturing the Texas Rancher's Heart*
Book 2: *The Rancher Risks It All*
Book 3: *The Bronc Rider Takes a Fall*
Book 4: *The Sheriff and the Cowgirl*

The Blood Brothers series

Book 1: *True Blue Cowboy*
Book 2: *Homeward Bound, Cowboy*
Book 3: *Her Secret Cowboy*

The Texas Lawmen series

Book 1: *Beware the Ranger*
Book 2: *The Lawman's Apache Moon*
Book 3: *Along Came a Ranger*
Book 4: *The Sheriff's Christmas Angels*

Available now at your favorite online retailer!

About the Author

Born and raised in the Lone Star state of Texas, Debra grew up among horses, cowboys, wide open spaces, and real Texas Rangers. Pride in her state and ancestry knows no bounds and it is these heroes and heroines she loves to write about the most. She also draws upon a variety of life experiences including working with abused children, caring for baby animals at a major zoo, and planning high-end weddings (ah, romance!).

Debra's real pride and joys, however, are her son, an aspiring film actor, and a daughter with aspirations to join the Federal Bureau of Investigation (more story ideas!). When she isn't busy writing about tall Texans and feisty heroines, she can be found cheering on her Texas Tech Red Raiders, or heading off on another cruise adventure. She read her first romance, Janet Dailey's *Fiesta San Antonio*, over thirty years ago and became hooked on the genre. Writing contemporary western romance is both her passion and dream come true, and she hopes her books will bring smiles…and sighs…to all who believe in happily-ever-after's.

Thank you for reading

Home to the Cowboy's Arms

If you enjoyed this book, you can find more from all our great authors at TulePublishing.com, or from your favorite online retailer.

Printed in Dunstable, United Kingdom

70059185R00129